# THE TIME TRAVEL DIARIES
# ADVENTURE IN ATHENS

## CAROLINE LAWRENCE

First published in Great Britain in 2020 by
PICCADILLY PRESS
80–81 Wimpole St, London W1G 9RE
www.piccadillypress.co.uk

Text copyright © Roman Mysteries Ltd., 2020
Illustrations by Sara Mulvanny/agencyrush.com, 2020

A CIP catalogue record for this book is available from the British Library.

ISBN: 978-1-84812-847-7
*Also available as an ebook and in audio*

1

This book is typeset by Perfect Bound Ltd
Printed and bound in Great Britain by Clays Ltd, Elcograf S.p.A.

Piccadilly Press is an imprint of Bonnier Books UK
www.bonnierbooks.co.uk

*To Professor Armand D'Angour,*
*who kindly consulted on this book and*
*allowed himself to appear as a character in it.*

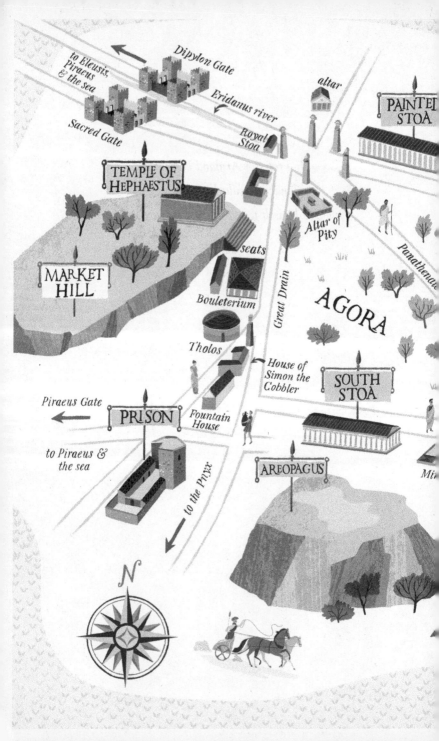

# ATHENS c.415 BC

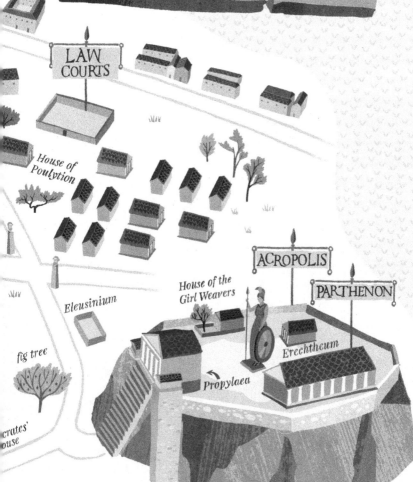

LAW COURTS

*House of Poulytion*

ACROPOLIS

PARTHENON

*House of the Girl Weavers*

*Eleusinium*

*Erechtheum*

*fig tree*

*Propylaea*

crates' ouse

# 1
# Fame at Last

When my best friend and I went back in time to track down the wisest man who ever lived, we only did it so we could be rich and famous.

It all started when we arrived back at school on the first day after the Easter holiday. We were fresh off the plane from a two-week language school in the Alban hills outside Rome and had taken an Uber straight from the airport.

As we came into the school cafeteria halfway through lunch, everybody fell silent and looked in our direction with admiring whispers and nudges. Having been a nerdy geek all my life, I naturally assumed it was for someone else. I turned around to see if some superstar had come in behind us. But it was just the two of us: me and Dinu.

I raised my eyebrows at Dinu. He's a big Romanian kid who used to be a bit of a bully.

Now he's my best mate.

'What's going on?' he asked me in ancient Greek, the language we had been studying intensively for the past fortnight. 'Is it because we're in ordinary clothes?'

'I don't think so,' I replied. 'Maybe they found out what we did at the beginning of the year?'

'No way,' he said. 'And it wouldn't impress them even if they knew.'

'You're probably right.'

As I helped myself to mac and cheese with green beans I studied Dinu, who was going for a baked potato with all the trimmings.

He looked good. The Italian sun had lightened his hair from butter blond to lemon blond. His white T-shirt showed off a good tan and nice muscle definition.

'Maybe they're staring because we look good?'

Dinu puffed out his chest. '*I* look good, you mean.' He gave me a teasing grin. 'You only look good to people with no dentists or proper doctors.'

I sighed. Dinu was right. Sure, I have good teeth, clear skin and shiny hair but so does practically everybody else in twenty-first-century London. I'm the smallest kid in my year group and have the voice of a choirboy.

Even my Roman suntan couldn't make me cool.

So why the admiring looks?

Dinu and I set off for the table at the far end of the cafeteria, where our friends from Latin club usually sat.

Everyone was beaming at us, from the big Year Twelve football players to the woke kids in Year Ten to the little Year Seven environmentalists. Even the mean girls in Year Eight looked interested.

'Why is everyone smiling at us?' asked Dinu, still speaking in ancient Greek.

'*Oo-den oy-dah*,' I replied. I know nothing.

'Dinu! Alex! Come sit!' called one of the Mean Girls.

Her name was Chastity. Her dad was a pop star who didn't believe in private education and she was the prettiest, meanest girl at Wandsworth Academy. She had blue dip-dyed hair and a butterfly tattoo on her neck.

Yup. A real tattoo.

Even the teachers were afraid of her.

I slowed down. 'Want to sit with them?'

'I guess?' Dinu replied.

I let him sit next to Chastity and I put my tray of food next to Kiana's. Kiana is half Jamaican with tight black curls, tawny skin and golden eyes. She is what my gran would call *petite*, which is French for small but perfectly formed.

'What language were you two guys speaking?' asked Chastity, running her hand through her blue-tipped hair.

'Um, ancient Greek,' I said. 'We've just been on an intensive course in a *palazzo* outside Rome.'

I braced myself for mocking laughter. Instead the third girl, Maude, sighed. 'Ooh, I love the way you say *palazzo*.'

3

'It's Italian for "palace",' I said. My voice came out squeakier than I would have liked, but none of them seemed to notice. I babbled on: 'It was this mansion with frescoes on the walls and massive formal gardens and a view of Rome.'

Chastity leaned forward. 'Is it true that you were being sponsored by Mannasoft Games?'

'Just for commenting on YouTube?' added Kiana.

'Yes.' Dinu looked pleased. 'We posted a walk-through of their latest platform game and they liked it. So now we're consultants.'

'Mannasoft Games are the coolest,' said Maude. The pink tips on her hair matched the colour of her lips.

'You like computer games set in the ancient world?' I said, frozen with a forkful of pasta halfway to my mouth.

'Duh,' said Chastity, and Maude said, 'Obvs.'

'Then you might like to know,' said Dinu importantly, 'that we are consulting with them on their next game too. It's set in ancient Athens. That's why they sent us to Italy. To learn ancient Greek.'

'I thought they spoke Latin in Italy,' said Maude.

'No, Italian,' said Chastity. 'Latin is a dead language.'

I had to pinch myself. The coolest girls in our year group were discussing ancient Greek and Latin.

In my mind I was screaming: *What on earth happened in the two weeks we were off-grid?*

# 2
# Mean Girls

I stared at Dinu and he stared at me. We couldn't believe the Wandsworth Academy Mean Girls were interested in the ancient-Greek language school we had attended over Easter.

'Um . . . Chastity is right,' I said. 'They do speak Italian in Italy. But this was a special place for learning two dead languages: Latin or ancient Greek.'

'Say something in ancient Greek!' breathed Maude.

Dinu grinned and leaned forward. '*You're so hot you could burn down Troy.*'

'Dinu!' I hissed in Greek. 'Be serious!'

'What did he say?' asked Maude, turning her baby-blue gaze on me.

Thinking quickly I replied, 'He said you are as beautiful as Helen of Troy, whose face launched a thousand ships. You all are!' I added hastily, looking at each of them in turn.

Chastity and Kiana rolled their eyes at each other, but Maude giggled.

I took a big bite of pasta but my throat was dry with panic and I started choking. For a terrible moment I was afraid I might die right in front of them, but their gently patting hands and a big mouthful of water helped get it down.

Dinu rolled his eyes. His meaning was clear: *I can't take you anywhere.*

I dabbed my watering eyes with a paper napkin. Could I *be* any more of a geek?

And yet the Mean Girls were still being nice to me.

'Hey, you guys should come to a party at my house this Saturday,' said Chastity. 'My parents are out for the night and we're going to have a multiplayer session of the best platform game ever.'

Kiana winked. 'I think you know which one.'

I nearly fainted. The most beautiful girls in Year Eight inviting us to play a computer game? Something was definitely wrong in the universe.

Somehow, Dinu and I managed to make it through the rest of lunch. We told them about the trip we'd taken to an Etruscan graveyard and a Greek comedy we'd performed and a thunderstorm over Rome. When the bell rang the girls all stood up and gave us radiant smiles as they took their trays.

They left me and Dinu sitting stunned.

'What just happened?' I asked him.

'No idea.'

'Have we come back to a parallel universe?' I said. 'Shall we call Mr Posh?'

Back in January, when Dinu and I had come back from a top-secret trip, we had been debriefed by a government official we called Mr Posh. He told us to alert him if we noticed anything about our world that was different from when we had left. Over the following days, weeks and months neither of us had seen anything that seemed wrong. But now I was beginning to wonder.

The cafeteria was emptying out and we were just about to take our trays when Dinu's younger sister plonked herself down beside him, opposite me.

'I don't suppose either of you have a clue what's going on, do you?' she said.

Eleven-year-old Crina was going for the eco-radical look with green spectacles and her mouse-brown hair in braids. If Dinu got the looks in his family, she got the brains.

'Nope,' I agreed. 'Not a clue.'

Crina looked over the top of her green-rimmed glasses. 'Have either of you heard of Bluzie Steenberg?'

'That singer you like with the pink hair?' said Dinu.

I said, 'The one who produces music out of her garage in northern California?'

Crina nodded. 'Her hair is purple this week,' she said. 'But yes.'

7

'So?' I said. 'What does she have to do with us?'

'Apparently Bluzie is a bit of a geek who plays computer games. You know that YouTube commentary you did about the game set in Roman London? She loves it and even mentions the two of you by name in her latest song.'

'You're joking,' I said.

'Nope. The song's called "Take Me Back", and there's a line that goes "Take me back Alex and Dinu; I'll go anywhere with you . . ."'

Dinu was grinning like an idiot but I still couldn't get my head around it. 'We're suddenly cool because a sixteen-year-old girl wrote a song about our YouTube commentary on a computer game?'

Crina rolled her eyes. 'Bluzie has fifty million followers and thousands of people sample her songs on that music app. Everybody loves her, from toddlers to teens to grannies. Can you think of any other reason why everybody in the school would think you're cool?'

Dinu and I looked at each other.

'You don't think it's because you went back in time, do you?' she said.

My jaw dropped and Dinu's blue eyes bugged out.

Somehow his annoying little sister had discovered our closely guarded secret.

But how?

# 3
# Take Me Back

Last year Dinu and I were kind of thrown together because we were both new at Wandsworth Academy.

I had joined the school in September and he arrived shortly before Christmas. Not only did we see each other on weekdays but also on Sundays because we happen to attend the same church in Battersea: the Greek Orthodox Church of Saint Nektarios, patron saint of bees. I go to that church because I live with my gran, who is Greek. Dinu's family goes because the priests there do part of the service in Romanian.

Maybe because he knew me from church, or maybe because he was the biggest in our year group and I'm the smallest, Dinu started mugging me for my crisps every morning.

So things were looking grim for me at the start of winter term.

Then a mad bazillionaire named Solomon Daisy offered

me five million pounds to go back in time to find a girl from Roman London. I only had to follow three rules:

1. Naked you go and naked you must return.
2. Drink, don't eat.
3. As little interaction as possible.

Of course I took the job. Wouldn't you? That kind of money can buy a very nice two-bedroom, two-bathroom flat in central London with enough left over for a private school with small classes and no bullies.

But going through the time portal was pretty horrible, especially when Dinu crashed through after me. Not knowing the rules, he came through on a full stomach. That was when we discovered the messy consequences of ignoring rule number two: *Drink, don't eat.*

At first I was furious at being saddled with Dinu the bully, but it turns out that being sent back nearly two thousand years is a good bonding experience. On the mean streets of Roman London, we realised we needed to rely on each other.

After we got back, I started spending time with Dinu up at the common. Kicking a football with him and some of the other Saturday-afternoon boys, I found my niche as a centre midfield defender while Dinu 'parked the bus' in goal.

I think we were good for each other at school too. He stopped being a bully, and the other kids stopped calling me Wimpy.

He even joined Latin club. Though that was mainly for

the free salt-and-vinegar crisps Miss Forte gives us at the end of each session.

Sometimes I would catch kids looking at us as we walked down the hall together. I knew they were wondering what on earth had brought us together. One minute Dinu had been mugging me for my crisps, and the next we were mates.

Nobody knew why we had suddenly become friends.

But now it appeared someone *did* know what had brought us together.

And that person was Dinu's annoying little sister. She was sitting there with a 'Protect the Planet' pin on the lapel of her blazer, peering at me over her eco-friendly glasses.

'Dinu!' I hissed. 'You weren't supposed to tell anybody!'

'I didn't! I swear it!'

'Dinu didn't tell me.' Crina raised her eyebrows at me. 'You did.'

'Me?' I squeaked.

'Yeah. A few weeks ago, before you and Dinu went to Italy, I heard the two of you talking in his bedroom.'

'Hey!' said Dinu. 'There's no way you could have heard us unless you had your head pressed against the wall.'

Crina gave us a smug smile. 'Of course I didn't press my head against the wall. Sound carries much better when you put an empty glass between your ear and the wall.'

Dinu called her a name in Romanian.

'Language!' tutted Crina, as cool as mint ice cream.

'Have you told anyone?' I said. 'Listen, Crina, you can't tell anybody else.'

She sighed. 'Of course I haven't told anybody else. And I promise I never will.'

'Thank God!' I breathed.

'On one condition.' She leaned forward.

'No conditions!' said Dinu between clenched teeth. 'Absolutely not.'

Crina ignored him and kept her beady brown eyes fixed on me. 'My condition is this: next time you go back in time, you take me with you.'

I thought about this for a moment. Then I allowed myself a slow grin. 'Sure.' I folded my arms and leaned back. 'Next time we go back we'll take you with us.' I paused for emphasis. 'Only there won't *be* a next time! The guy who sent us back is in prison for the rest of his life. And I'm pretty sure they threw away the key.'

'So beat it, little sister.' Dinu ran a comb through his hair. 'We're popular now. We can't be seen with the likes of you.'

Crina glared at us. 'You know your problem? You want to be rich and famous. But you should care about things that really matter.'

'What?' I scoffed. 'Like saving the world?'

'Exactly!' She stood up and glared down at us. 'Enjoy your moment of popularity. It won't last. As soon as Bluzie brings out a new song you'll be history.'

I looked at Dinu and said in ancient Greek, 'I think we should take your sister's advice. Let's enjoy every moment. Play with the Mean Girls this Saturday?'

'*Carpe diem!*' said Dinu, and gave me a fist bump.

I laughed at the expression on Crina's face. She had no idea what we were saying and steam was practically coming out of the top of her mousy head.

'You two think you're so clever,' she growled. Then she stomped off.

'We are clever,' I said to Dinu.

Later that day we felt rich as well as clever: Mannasoft Games emailed, congratulating us on our mention in Bluzie's song and offering to fly us and our families to Athens for a two-week all-expenses-paid luxury break at the start of the summer holiday.

And at the weekend, when I found myself squished in on a couch next to Kiana as we played *Back to Londinium* with Dinu and Chastity, I felt like a superhero.

It was the best thing ever.

No wonder everybody craves popularity, fame and fortune.

# 4

# Play-Doh's Dialogues

Gran once told me that everybody in the world gets fifteen minutes of fame at some point during their life. I have no idea who said it.

I guess they're not famous any more.

Anyway, Dinu and I got way more than fifteen minutes. We enjoyed almost a whole month of celebrity. Bluzie's song stayed in the charts and our Mannasoft Games walk-through of *Back to Londinium* soon had over three million hits.

We went to parties and sat with the cool kids and even our teachers were nicer to us than usual.

For the school's summer talent show Dinu and I did a kind of stand-up comic routine where I'm the clever geeky one and Dinu's cool but thick. It was a spoof of our YouTube commentary but instead of Roman London we pretended to go back to when our teachers were young: caveman times. Geddit?

We got a standing ovation.

The adoration made me feel so good that I even grew a few millimetres taller. I was still the shortest kid in Year Eight but at least it meant I was now almost eye to eye with my girlfriend Kiana.

Yes: girlfriend.

Thanks to a mention on one of the most downloaded pop songs in the history of the world, I had a girlfriend.

It's true that Kiana and I didn't have many interests in common and that she only allowed me to hold her hand when we were at school and that she hardly ever came to my house and when she did she usually rolled her eyes at my suggestions of computer games to play.

But still . . .

A girlfriend!

I wasn't complaining.

When I walked down the corridor I got fist bumps and nods and envious smiles from my delightful fellow students. How could I ever have thought of leaving Wandsworth Academy?

After a month or so our popularity started to fade a little. Kiana always seemed to have an excuse when I invited her over to play a computer game and she stopped letting me hold her hand at school.

But then the ads on our YouTube commentary started to pay out, and this meant that Dinu and I had extra pocket money. We could afford Air Force One trainers and Off White backpacks. And when I bought Kiana a silver heart bracelet with 'K&A' engraved on it, she let me hold her hand in public again.

The only bug in my soup was Dinu's pesky sister Crina, with her annoying green glasses and angry lapel pins.

'I'm not going to Athens with the rest of you this summer,' she said every time I went round for dinner. 'I don't want to leave a massive carbon footprint.'

'If you're not coming to Athens with us, then why are you reading Plato's dialogues?' said Dinu one Friday evening as he spooned sour cream on his mamaliga.

Crina's cheeks grew pink. 'How did you know that?'

'You're not the only one who can spy,' he said with a smirk.

'I love Plato,' said five-year-old Mari. 'Pink is my favourite colour.'

'I think she means "Play-Doh",' said Crina. She leaned forward and smiled at her little sister. 'Plato was a famous philosopher in ancient Greece. He wrote about Socrates, another philosopher.'

Mari held up Dodo, the teddy bear she takes everywhere. 'Dodo has flossy fur.'

Dinu snorted and Crina gave him a stern look. 'Not flossy fur,' she said gently. 'Philosopher. That's a person who thinks about the meaning of life. And a dialogue just means talking about something.'

I looked at Crina. 'So why *are* you reading Plato's dialogues, if you're not going to Athens with us?'

Mrs Balan said, 'Of course she is going. Is rude to say no to this very kind invitation.'

Unlike her three kids, whose English was almost perfect after less than a year in the country, Mrs Balan still had a heavy Romanian accent.

I liked her. She was pretty and petite with big brown eyes. Sometimes she hugged me and kissed my forehead, just like my mum used to do.

I felt a bit sorry for Mrs Balan because Mr Balan was away so much, working on a construction site. 'Will your husband be able to come with us?' I asked. 'He's invited too.'

'I don't think so,' replied Mrs Balan. 'He still works hard on those apartments.'

I had only met Dinu's dad once, at Easter. He was tall and muscular with thinning blond hair and a jaw like a superhero. He always said he would try to show up for Dinu's football matches or to see Crina play clarinet in the school talent show. But work came first and he rarely made it.

When Mrs Balan said Mr Balan probably couldn't come to Athens with us everyone looked sad except Dinu, who scowled.

But I knew he was hurt rather than angry. He once told me that when he lived in Romania he and his dad used to spend much more time together. Quickly trying to change the subject, I turned back to Crina. 'You still haven't told me why you're reading Plato.'

Crina raised her eyebrows and looked at me over the top of her green glasses. 'You know very well why.'

But to be honest, I had no clue.

# 5
# First Class

'Ahhh! This is the life,' I said to Dinu as I looked out the window of BA flight 632 and sipped an iced Coke. It was the first week of the summer holiday and we were on our way to Athens. Our plane was cruising at around 35,000 feet somewhere over the Alps.

Dinu nodded. 'What makes it especially good is that we're in business class and my annoying sister has to sit back there!' He jerked his thumb towards the economy section of the plane.

I suppressed a twinge of guilt. Dinu's mum and my gran were also back there. And of course Dinu's cute little sister Mari.

'I hear economy isn't so bad.' I was telling myself as much as him. I finished my Coke, put on my eye mask and plugged in my earphones.

I was dozing to Bluzie's song 'Take Me Back' when I was

rudely awakened by a tap on my forearm. I pulled out my earbuds, lifted my eye mask and squinted up at the person lit from behind.

'How's first class?' Crina stood in the aisle with her arms folded. 'I hope you're enjoying it.'

I beamed up at her. 'Loving it. How's cattle class?'

She sighed. 'We've got screaming babies all around us. Literally surround sound. Wanna trade?'

'No, thank you,' I said, putting my mask back over my eyes. 'We're the VIPs.'

I couldn't see her any more, but I could feel her standing there, glowering down at us.

'Stop moaning,' I heard Dinu tell her. 'We only have another hour before we land and then you'll be in a luxury five-star hotel. All expenses paid and everything. And all because of us. So be grateful.'

'Do you at least have some earplugs I can borrow?' came her voice.

'Here,' said Dinu. 'Take this comfort pack. It has earplugs, socks and an eye mask.'

'Thanks,' she muttered.

'Sorry, miss, but you can't be up here in first class,' I heard a female member of the cabin crew say.

'All right, all right. I'm going.'

I couldn't help giving a wicked grin.

At Athens airport we found one of those golf-cart things

to take us to baggage claim. Dinu and I let Gran, his mum and the girls ride in the cart with our carry-ons while we went on foot. It was a long way but it felt good to stretch our legs. I walked on the travelator while Dinu jogged along the one going the opposite direction. Then we traded places. By the time we reached the baggage claim, laughing and slightly out of breath, they were waiting patiently with our suitcases.

Like our entourage.

Sweet.

'This must be what it's like to be rich and famous,' I whispered to Dinu.

But outside in the arrivals lounge my good mood deflated like a month-old balloon. 'They told me there would be someone here to meet us with our names on a placard.'

'And where are the screaming fans?' said Dinu with a grin.

People were swirling around, crying out greetings and hugging relatives.

'I'll bet pop stars and millionaires don't have to hang around for their rides,' I grumbled. 'Where *is* he?'

'Maybe over there?' said Dinu. 'By that kiosk?'

As I looked at the sweet stall where Dinu was pointing, I noticed a skinny guy in a floppy canvas sunhat and orange mirrored sunglasses facing our way. When he saw me notice him, he moved behind a stand of magazines.

'I think we're being watched,' I muttered to Dinu.

'By Bluzie fans?' He looked around eagerly.

'Dunno,' I replied.

'Act cool,' said Dinu. 'In case they're filming us.'

At that moment a stocky guy in a charcoal-grey suit and aviator sunglasses appeared before us.

'Alex Pappas, Dinu Balan and family?' he growled.

When we nodded he held up a placard with MANNASOFT GAMES scrawled on it. 'I am Stavros, your driver. Please come with me.'

Before I could ask where he had been, he grabbed a couple of our suitcases and led the way out into a blast of late afternoon heat.

'Look, Mummy!' said little Mari. 'A stretchy car.'

'Woohoo!' Dinu punched the air. 'A limo!'

Stavros opened the door for Gran and Mrs Balan to get in first. 'It has a mini-fridge with complimentary champagne, Coke and Pringles.'

Crina scowled as she slumped in the leather seat. 'Coke is poison,' she said. 'So are all those other processed foods. And I can't believe all six of us have just flown to Greece and now we're in this giant car. We're leaving a massive carbon footprint. We should have at least taken the airport bus.'

I glanced at Dinu and he just rolled his eyes: we understood each other perfectly.

As I cracked open a can of Coke I resolved to avoid Dinu's annoying little sister as much as possible during this holiday.

Fate was having a good laugh at me just then.

# 6
# Five-Star Athens

The five-star Athens Acropole Hotel was well posh.

Dinu and I had our own massive room between my gran's single room and the big suite occupied by Dinu's mum and his two sisters. There were connecting doors but we immediately locked them on our side. Crina was less than pleased to have to share with her mum and little Mari, but that was her problem, not mine. Our room boasted a balcony with a view of the Acropolis, a queen-sized bed each and a huge plasma TV, complete with console and games.

'Hey!' exclaimed Dinu. 'They have an alpha version of *Back to Athens*! And oh my God – look! *Ancient Greek Assassins!*'

'Aren't we supposed to go up to the roof terrace for some introductory banquet?' I said. 'Remember? Stavros was telling us about it in the limo.'

But my protests faded away when the first screen of Mannasoft Games' *Back to Athens* came up.

'Wicked!' said Dinu. 'Look at those graphics. Right up there with *Ancient Greek Assassins*!'

'How do you know? You said you've never played *Assassins*.'

'I haven't. But I've watched walk-throughs on YouTube.'

'Dinu, are you riding a chariot through the streets of Athens? I don't think that was allowed.'

'Make a note then, dude,' said Dinu. 'That's what we're here to do.'

We were deeply immersed in the ancient world when we were brought back to twenty-first-century Athens by a ringing phone. It took me a few seconds to find it on one of the bedside tables.

'Hello?' I said.

'Alex, where are you?' came Gran's voice. 'We're all waiting for you up on the roof. They've laid out a special banquet for us with musicians and waiters dressed in ancient clothing and everything.'

'Sorry, Gran! We'll be right up!'

'Don't forget to wash your hands. I might sniff them to check.'

The bathroom was amazing. The walls were shiny white marble veined with black. The taps looked made of gold and were shaped like dolphins. There were twin hand basins of black marble with a bowl of little shell-shaped soaps nearby.

'Hey, Alex!' said Dinu as I dried my hands on a fluffy white towel. 'What's this?'

He was pointing at a low white basin next to the toilet.

'I think it's called a bidet,' I said.

'Bee-day?'

'Yeah. B-I-D-E-T. I'm not quite sure what it's for.'

'Maybe it's for washing socks and pants,' said Dinu.

I looked around at the marble walls and the gilded dolphin-shaped spouts. 'I don't think people who stay here need to handwash their own underwear.'

But Dinu was already out the door on his way to the lift.

I dropped the towel and gave my hands a sniff. Coconut. Gran would approve.

Up on the roof terrace, you could see the ancient ruins on the Acropolis above us, glowing pink in the setting sun. It was still hot but there was a nice breeze up here. There was even a pool.

Then I spotted our table. I was surprised to see that the six of us were the only diners up there. We were outnumbered by four musicians, a woman singer and three waiters. The waiters looked like Greek gods who spent too much time at the gym and wanted everyone to know it; they wore sleeveless mini-tunics.

Gran and Mrs Balan and the two girls were all dressed up. Even Crina. She had unplaited her hair, left off her glasses and put on some eyeliner. She had changed from her Extinction Rebellion T-shirt and jeans into a bright turquoise dress that looked like an ancient Greek tunic.

I was about to tell her she looked nice when she said, 'Wow! You really made an effort, didn't you?' Her voice was heavy with sarcasm.

'You could at least have put on a fresh T-shirt, Alex,' said my gran.

I looked down at my pale blue T-shirt. It was smeared with Pringle dust and splashes of Coke from where the can had fizzed over.

'We got distracted,' I said feebly, then noticed that Dinu had changed into a fresh shirt. 'Traitor!' I muttered under my breath.

We had an amazing feast of stuffed grape leaves and roast lamb and a bunch of other courses and then did traditional Greek line dancing, all except for little Mari, who fell asleep on a sun lounger by the pool. Even usually grumpy Crina joined in the dancing and seemed to be enjoying herself. She picked up the Zorba dance pretty quickly.

I realised I felt happier than I had in a long time, which surprised me because of all the popularity I'd been enjoying at school.

I'm not sure what time we went to bed, just that it was after midnight.

But I do remember the moment Dinu woke me up.

'Alex,' he groaned, 'I don't feel so good.'

I squinted at the glowing numbers of the bedside clock. 'Dinu! It's four in the morning! Go back to sleep.'

'Urgh!' he moaned. 'I think I'm going to be sick.'

'Oh, Dinu!' I gave a deep sigh as he stumbled across the dark bedroom towards the bathroom.

But a moment later my own stomach was churning and I also felt a horrible urge to throw up.

I ran into the bathroom. The brilliant light showed me Dinu with his head over the toilet, heaving.

I looked around desperately for somewhere to be sick.

Then I spotted the bidet. I'm still not sure what its real purpose is, but all that night it served me well.

# 7
# Not Bill and Ted

I t turned out that everybody else had been struck down too. We found out when a doctor arrived at our door around nine in the morning. He was a round-faced man with excellent English. He told us that we must be suffering from food poisoning because everyone who had been at the banquet was ill: Gran, Mrs Balan and the girls.

He couldn't say if it was the grape leaves or the lamb, or maybe the honey pastries, but he told us not to eat anything and to drink plenty of fluids, preferably water.

'I've seen this before,' he said. 'The best treatment is to avoid food for a full forty-eight hours. If you start eating before it's completely out of your body, the sickness could recur.' He raised dark eyebrows at us. 'Do you think you can do that?'

We both nodded.

'Some holiday,' I grumbled when he had left.

'It's a great holiday,' said Dinu. 'I have a bed the size of a small room and a plasma TV.'

So Dinu and I stayed in our beds that whole day. Our room was the perfect temperature and also nice and dim after we closed the blinds against the fierce sun.

At first we tried watching TV, but the selection of programmes was bizarre. All the movies were about Greek myths or heroes. Then there were about a hundred documentaries about the history of Athens and how democracy was born here, and the building of the Acropolis and so forth. We watched some of those until I found a Blu-Ray of *Bill and Ted's Excellent Adventure*.

We both laughed at the bit where Bill and Ted have to go back to get an ancient Greek philosopher named Socrates.

In the movie, Bill pronounces the philosopher's name '*Soak Rates*', and then reads out a quote from their guide book: 'The only true wisdom consists of knowing that you know nothing.' Bill and Ted grin at each other and say, 'That's us, dude!'

Dinu and I both dozed off and missed the end of the movie, but we felt better for our nap.

'I could eat something,' said Dinu, grabbing the menu for room service.

'Me too,' I said. 'But we're not supposed to for another day and a half. Doctor's orders.'

Dinu put down the menu and picked up the *Ancient Greek*

*Assassins* box. He waggled it temptingly. 'Wimpy?'

'I don't think Gran would approve of me playing such a violent game. And don't call me "Wimpy".'

'Don't be wimpy, Wimpy.'

And when I hesitated, he said, 'Come on. It will take your mind off not eating.'

I picked up the box and studied it.

A sticker read: 'Special Complimentary Athens Acropole Edition – not for resale.'

A black-and-white label read: 'Mature Seventeen Plus. Blood and Gore. Intense Violence. Strong Language. Parental Advisory!'

'No,' I said. 'This is not *Bill and Ted's Excellent Adventure*. Absolutely not.'

We played *Ancient Greek Assassins* for three or four hours.

It was just the Athens section of the game so we couldn't go to Sparta or Crete or anywhere else, but we didn't mind too much. The ancient city had tons of different districts and we kept finding new parts.

My favourite bit was killing all the guards in the Prytaneum so you can get *ostraka*, the broken pieces of pottery with names of unpopular politicians scratched on them.

Dinu loved the climbing parts. He never took a ramp or the stairs if he could climb. Like a sticky monkey, he scaled smooth temple columns, the sheer side of the Acropolis and even the colossal statue of Athena.

'Whoa! Look at this!' he cried as he reached Athena's crest. Suddenly the viewpoint shifted and the music swelled and a soaring hawk showed us a 360-degree view of Athens from high up.

'*Excellent!*' I said, imitating Ted from the movie.

A tap on one of the connecting doors brought us both back to the present. I was surprised to see it was dark outside.

We hastily turned off the TV and shoved the box in a drawer. Then Dinu opened the door to reveal Gran looking pale in a paisley kaftan. Crina stood beside her in shorts and a lime-green T-shirt that said *What Would Greta Do*?

Gran gave us a feeble smile. 'Poor little Mari had to go to hospital so they could give her a drip, and obviously her mum went too. That leaves Crina on her own. Is it all right if she hangs out with you two?'

# 8
# Limo Surprise

Crina had a pleading look in her big brown puppy-dog eyes.

But I wasn't fooled. There was no way I wanted her to spend even five minutes in our room. She'd make us watch something educational or politically correct.

Or both.

I looked at Dinu and he looked at me.

As usual, we understood each other perfectly.

'We're actually still feeling kind of sick,' I lied.

'Yeah,' said Dinu. 'In fact, I think I'm gonna hurl.' He made a big thing of running to the bathroom.

Crina's smile faded and she glared at me.

I could tell she wasn't fooled.

'I don't want to be in here anyway,' she muttered. 'It smells of boy socks and sick.'

'This room *is* a bit stuffy.' Gran went and opened the

blinds and then the window. 'You've got a lovely view of the Acropolis,' she said.

Then she went back and put her arm around Crina's shoulders, 'Come on, sweetheart. Let's watch a nice film. I have a good selection in my room. I'll make us a cup of herbal tea.'

They started to go but then Gran turned back. 'Why don't we all meet upstairs by the pool tomorrow?' she said. 'We can sip herbal tea and stay cool under parasols. Around ten or eleven in the morning?'

'OK,' I said, trying to make my voice feeble. 'See you tomorrow. Feel better soon.'

Crina narrowed her eyes at me but Gran was already guiding her out of the doorway and I heard her say, 'There's a fun rom-com called *It's All Greek*.'

As soon as the door shut Dinu peeped out of the bathroom. 'Is it safe?'

I gave him a thumbs-up and we spent another few hours exploring virtual Athens and slaughtering Corinthian spies.

We both slept well, considering we had been couch potatoes all day.

The next morning I was woken by the sun streaming through our window and the sound of the shower coming from the bathroom.

When I opened my eyes I saw Dinu getting dressed.

'What are you doing?' I asked.

'Come on, dude. It's a beautiful morning. Have a shower – quick – and then we can go for a walk. I have to find salt-and-vinegar crisps. Or maybe Pringles.'

'You heard the doctor,' I said, stretching. 'Nothing to eat until sundown this evening or better yet tomorrow at breakfast.'

But a shower sounded good.

I got up, padded into the bathroom and recoiled at the smell. 'Maybe I will go for a walk with you,' I called. 'If we go out, housekeeping can make up the room.' I wrinkled my nose. 'And clean the bidet.'

A shower made me feel much better. I dressed in jeans and a clean T-shirt. Then I found a notepad on the hotel desk and slipped a note under the door to Gran's room: *GONE FOR SHORT WALK. DON'T WORRY, WE WON'T EAT. SEE YOU LATER BY POOL. A.*

Then I flipped over the *DO NOT DISTURB* sign on the outside of the door so that it read *PLEASE CLEAN THE ROOM.*

A few minutes later revolving doors swung us out of the hotel lobby into dazzling sunlight. It wasn't even nine o'clock, but it felt as hot as Vesuvius out there. I could see a layer of smog over Athens, and smell it too. The traffic was manic.

I felt a bit dizzy and was about to plead with Dinu to go back and sit in the lobby, when a stretch limo pulled up.

'Hey,' said Dinu. 'It's Stavros from yesterday.'

34

Before I could reply, a door at the back opened.

'Alex! Dinu! What a coincidence!' said a familiar voice.

I glanced into the shadowy interior of the car and my jaw dropped.

The man in the back of the limo was a big guy, not to say obese. The last time I'd seen him, he was being handcuffed by police in the underground site of a temple to Mithras seven metres below the streets of London.

'Solomon Daisy!' My voice came out way too high. 'You're supposed to be in prison for the rest of your life.'

'Oh my God!' Dinu stared at him, bug-eyed. 'Did you break out of jail?'

And I said, 'What are you doing in Athens?'

But even as I said it, I knew.

He wanted to send me back to the past.

# 9

# Socrates Cafe

'My clever lawyers found a legal loophole,' explained Solomon Daisy half an hour later as he nibbled some baklava, the famous honey pastry of Greece. 'Apparently there's no law against time travel. So as you see, I am a free man.'

We were sitting at a table in the Socrates Cafe, which was an oasis of coolness beneath some big canvas parasols and leafy trees. Solomon Daisy was dressed in his usual clothes: plus-sized jeans and a grey T-shirt stretched across his generous belly.

He had lured us there with the promise of ice-cold Coke, which he claimed was good for an upset stomach.

'There is no way I'm going back in time again.' I sat back and folded my arms. 'We only came with you because we have a few things we wanted to say to you.'

'Like, time travel is no fun,' said Dinu.

'Like, you told me going through the portal would be like a roller coaster,' I said. 'But it's more like getting the bends. All your skin cells fizz like crazy, your ears ring and your eyes are stuck together.'

'And you throw up, or poop out anything left in your stomach,' added Dinu.

'Yes, we knew that.' Daisy licked some honey off his chubby fingers. 'That's why we made Alex fast for sixty hours before going through.'

'Sixty hours?' echoed Dinu in disbelief.

'It's only two and a half days,' said Daisy. 'You survived, didn't you, Alex?'

'Oh my God!' I leaned forward. 'The banquet last night! I'll bet you bribed the hotel doctor to put something in our food so our stomachs would be empty.'

He held up both hands, palms forward, and had the decency to look sheepish.

'You planned for us to get sick?' said Dinu. 'My little sister's in hospital!'

I grabbed Dinu's arm. 'I'll bet he's behind our trip to Italy. Was that all a trick to get us to learn ancient Greek?'

Before Daisy could answer, another thought hit me like a sledgehammer. 'Wait! Do you own Mannasoft Games?'

Daisy beamed at me over the tops of his glasses. 'Clever boy. That's why you're perfect for the job.'

'That explains the alpha version of *Back to Athens*, plus all the DVDs and guide books in our room. You were secretly preparing me to go.'

'Not just you, Alex. Both of you.'

Dinu nearly choked on a sip of Coke.

'You want me to go too?'

'Of course.' He beamed. 'You two make a great team.'

'There is no way I am going through that portal again!' I sat back in my chair.

'Me neither.' Dinu also sat back.

'Of course you are!' said Daisy cheerfully. 'Can you guess who I want you to find?'

'We just told you. We're not going back!'

'This guy!' Ignoring our refusals, Solomon Daisy opened his battered briefcase and produced something like an action figure. Made of white plastic designed to resemble marble, it was a statuette of a snub-nosed balding bearded guy wearing a cloak and holding a walking stick.

It was a type of souvenir you could buy all over Athens.

Of course I knew who he was, even without the name of the Socrates Cafe looming behind Solomon Daisy.

'Socrates?' I took the souvenir and examined it. 'You want us to find Socrates?'

Solomon Daisy nodded happily.

'Why him?' Dinu took the figurine and flicked the top of his little walking stick. 'What's so great about Socrates?'

'Socrates was very possibly the wisest man who ever lived.'

'I thought he claimed to know nothing.' I said.

Solomon Daisy ignored this. 'The so-called Socratic problem,' he said, 'is one that people have been debating for millennia. And I mean that literally. For thousands of years people have been wondering what Socrates was really like. The only thing everyone agrees about is that he was absolutely unique.'

'But what is he to you?' Dinu handed back the figurine and took a swig of his Coke.

'Ever since I took a class in philosophy, I've been obsessed. All I want you to do is find him and observe him in action for a few hours, then report back to me.' He spread his chubby hands and beamed at us. 'If you can accomplish that simple mission, I'll give you ten million. Each.'

# 10
# Jeff and Geoff

When Daisy said the magic words 'ten million each', some Coke spurted out of Dinu's nose.

I handed him a paper napkin. As Dinu cleaned himself up he said, 'You'll pay us ten mil each?'

'Yup!'

'Pounds, dollars or euros?'

'Does it matter?' Solomon Daisy beamed.

'Easy, bro!' I said. 'He promised me five million in January but I've never seen a penny of it.'

'The agreed sum cleared your grandmother's bank account this morning.' Solomon Daisy took a sip of his tiny Greek coffee. 'Ask her if you don't believe me. And I swear I will pay you each ten million – all you have to do is go back for just a day or two and observe Socrates.'

He snapped his fingers. But instead of our waiter coming over, two men who had been sitting at another table stood up. One of them was the skinny guy in the floppy sunhat I had seen watching me at the airport. He and the other one, who was Asian, were wearing sunglasses. As they brought their chairs over I finally recognised them as the inventors of Solomon Daisy's time portal.

'It's Geoff and Jeff!' I said. 'They're out of jail too?'

'Of course,' said Solomon Daisy. 'Like I already told you, there's no law against time travel.'

As the two super-geeks plunked themselves down, I noticed ginger-haired Geoff with a G was sunburned and sweating; his orange-mirrored sunglasses kept slipping down his nose. The reason I hadn't recognised him at the airport was because he had shaved off his little beard.

Jeff with a J had adapted better to the heat. His hair was cut in the latest fashion and his black T-shirt looked more cool than geeky, even though it did have a small Batman logo over the heart. His sunglasses were Ray-Bans.

'Tell them your idea, boys,' commanded Daisy.

Cool Jeff gestured towards some nearby ruins. 'This place was called the Lyceum,' he said. 'It was a garden sanctuary to the god Apollo, and one of Socrates' favourite haunts. He liked to come here and discuss the meaning of life with other Athenians.'

'And do you see those ruins, right down there?' Sweaty Geoff pointed at some unremarkable remains of what looked like an ancient wall on the other side of the chain-link fence.

'That's the ruins of a fifth-century palaestra. Also known as a gymnasium, after the Greek word for "naked", because men exercised in the nude.'

Cool Jeff said, 'Technically the palaestra is the open courtyard in the gymnasium. We think it would be the perfect place for the time portal. Nice and sandy for a soft landing. Plus everybody else will be naked too.'

Daisy beamed at us. 'If Socrates isn't at the Lyceum, you'll probably find him in the Agora or just outside. He liked to hang out at Simon the Cobbler's shop.'

'Cobbler?' said Dinu. 'I don't know that word.'

'It means "shoemaker",' I said.

'Ah,' said Dinu. 'And the Agora is like an ancient shopping centre. Correct?'

'Correct. Some scholars call it the Market Square.' Daisy jerked his thumb over his shoulder. 'It's that way. Just north of the Acropolis. Socrates was a local celebrity, so finding him should be pretty straightforward.'

'What about the war between the Athenians and the Spartans?' asked Dinu. 'Wasn't that going on when Socrates was alive?'

'Bravo!' Solomon Daisy clapped his hands. 'You boys have been doing your research.

Dinu shrugged modestly. 'I'm very clever.'

'Bah!' I scoffed. 'You only know about it from playing *Ancient Greek Assassins*.'

'Don't worry about the war,' said Cool Jeff. 'We plan to send you back to the year 415 BC when the Athenians and Spartans had made a truce. It was called the Peace of Nicias.'

'Do the three rules still apply?' I asked.

'Afraid so!' Sweaty Geoff mopped his forehead with a hanky. 'Naked you go; drink, don't eat; and no interaction.'

'So will you do it?' Solomon Daisy leaned forward in his seat.

Dinu took a thoughtful swig of his Coke. Then he nodded. 'Sure. For ten million pounds, euros or dollars – I'm in. As long as Alex goes too.'

I was torn. On the one hand, that was a lot of money. But according to Daisy, I already had five mil in Gran's account. Did I really need more? But there was a bigger problem.

'What good is all that money if the universe goes kerblam?' I said.

'What do you mean?' Solomon Daisy took the last piece of baklava.

'Mr Posh told us if we interact too much there's a risk of the whole universe kersploding.'

'*Kersploding?!*' he echoed. 'Nonsense!' Crumbs of pastry flew out of Daisy's mouth. 'If time travel was going to upset the order of things, it would have done that already. As long as you keep interaction to a minimum, you should be fine.'

'*Should be fine?*' I echoed. 'That doesn't exactly fill me with confidence.'

Daisy took off his black-rimmed glasses and polished them with a paper napkin. 'In addition to the money, I can make you famous.'

'Really?! How?'

'I can put you and Dinu in *Back to Athens*.'

'In what way?'

'We'll model the avatars on you. I'll even call you Alexis and Dionysus. Everyone will know your faces. And this version is going to be available in VR too, natch. Once the game comes out, you can go around the world with Bluzie Steenberg and have walk-on parts in her concerts. Think of it. You'll have a bazillion followers on Insta, YouTube and TikTok. You'll be more famous than Jay-Z and Beyoncé put together. Maybe even more than the Rock and Ronaldo.'

I looked at Dinu and he looked at me.

I was thinking of the envious looks I got from other kids at school, and the way Kiana's cheek dimpled when she smiled at me.

'To fame and fortune?' said Dinu, lifting his Coke.

I took a deep breath and nodded. 'To fame and fortune!'

We bumped our cans in a toast.

# 11
# Kiss or Kick

I t was nearly midnight when the limo picked us up outside our hotel.

Dinu and I had spent the rest of the morning by the pool with Gran and Crina. Little Mari was still in hospital for observation. I felt a very sorry for her and a little angry at Solomon Daisy, but I told myself it would be worth it for Dinu's family when he was rich and famous.

Dinu and I had splashed around the pool to take our mind off our upcoming trip. Gran and Crina hardly went in the water at all. They spent most of the morning with their noses in books. Finally curiosity got the better of me and I swam over to see what Crina was reading.

'It's called *Athens on Five Drachmas a Day*,' she said. 'It's a kind of guidebook to ancient Athens. Apparently the drachma was the ancient version of the euro.'

My stomach turned over. It suddenly occurred to me that

I should be prepping for the trip, not trying to forget about it. If ancient Athens was anything like Roman London, I would want to achieve the objective then get back home as soon as possible.

I pulled myself out of the water and perched on the hot concrete edge of the pool. 'Can I borrow that?' I asked her.

'Sure.' She handed me the book and stood up. 'Your gran is taking me shopping anyway. Want to come?'

'No, thanks. We're good right here.'

But we didn't stay by the pool.

As soon as they left, we went back to our room to prepare. I read the book and Dinu played more *Ancient Greek Assassins*.

Later that afternoon I slipped a note under Gran's door, saying we had gone to sleep early so that we could wake up and eat as soon as possible the next day.

Of course Dinu and I wouldn't be doing any eating. We would be going back to the past.

We set an alarm for 11.30 p.m. and tried to sleep. But we were both too nervous and hungry to drop off.

Now, sitting in the dark limo, my empty stomach felt full of flapping pigeons and the palms of my hands were tingling.

I was having serious second thoughts about this.

Then I remembered the admiring looks on our first day back from Greek School and I multiplied it by a thousand. I imagined getting off a plane and being mobbed by hundreds of screaming girls. Sweet.

'What about my gran?' I asked Solomon Daisy as the limo moved through the dark streets of night-time Athens. 'When I went back to Roman London I told her I was going on a school trip. Won't she worry when she finds us gone?'

'We'll get the hotel doctor to tell her and Dinu's mum that the two of you are in quarantine. We'll assure them it's for observation only,' Daisy added quickly, 'and we'll tell them not to worry.'

I nodded. But I knew Gran would worry. So would Mrs Balan.

In the dark interior of the limo, Cool Jeff leaned forward. 'There's a slight problem with the timings,' he said. 'We can only turn on the palaestra portal late at night, when nobody is around. We have no idea what time of day you'll land, but if it's daytime at least you'll be naked like the others.'

'Because we can only turn on the portal once,' said Daisy, 'that means you'll have to stay at least twenty-four hours. But you accomplished your last mission in a day. I'm confident you can do it again. Whatever time of day or night it is when you arrive, just make sure you're back at the portal twenty-four hours later. Or forty-eight if it takes you longer.'

'Staying forty-eight hours would take forty-eight months off our life expectancy, right?' I said.

'Yes,' said Solomon Daisy. 'If you have to stay two days, that will be four years off the end of your life. So you'll live to be eighty instead of eighty-four. Not a big deal.'

Dinu frowned. 'But what if the portal gets broken and we are stuck in the past? Would we die after only a couple of weeks?'

Jeff with a J shook his head. 'We think it's returning from the past that takes its toll on the body. If for some unlikely reason you get stuck in the past, you should be able to live a normal-length life.'

'Assuming something else doesn't kill you,' added Geoff with a G.

I felt a bit sick. I had to put my head between my knees.

'You all right, Wimpy?' said Dinu.

Anger replaced nausea and I sat up and glared at him. 'Don't call me Wimpy!'

The glow of a street light was enough to show me his grin. I realised he was trying to make me angry, knowing it would distract me from what we were about to do.

'Damn!' muttered Cool Jeff as the car pulled up beside the Socrates Cafe. He was peering out the window.

At first I couldn't see what had upset him. The cafe was dark and closed.

'There are police all over the place!' exclaimed Solomon Daisy.

That was when I saw the light of a torch and two policemen by the chain-link entrance to the archaeological site.

Our driver – it was Stavros again – slid back a glass panel

separating us from him. 'This is a bad place at night,' he said over his shoulder. 'Drug dealers come here. Also, it's a big make-out place. Sometimes police do crack-down.'

'There goes Plan G,' said Cool Jeff.

'Plan G?' I echoed.

'G for Gymnasium,' said Sweaty Geoff.

Solomon Daisy turned to Cool Jeff. 'You two were supposed to do your research!' he said. 'Didn't you do a midnight recce?'

'Yeah, but there weren't any police here last night,' said Sweaty Geoff.

'It was totally deserted,' confirmed Cool Jeff.

'Too bad we don't know Athens as well as we know London,' sighed Daisy.

'I guess we'll have to call it off,' I said, with a sigh of relief.

'I didn't get where I am today,' said Solomon Daisy, 'by giving up easily. There must be another place to put the portal.'

'We need to find somewhere that is in exactly the same location as it was two and a half thousand years ago,' said Cool Jeff. 'Not just longitude and latitude—'

'But altitude,' we all said together.

'And empty,' Sweaty Geoff murmured. 'So the boys don't step into a big column or something.'

'Hey, guys?' said Dinu.

We all looked at him.

'I know a place we can go where we'll end up on the same level as in ancient times.'

We all stared at him some more.

He pointed. 'Right up there.'

We all leaned over to his side to see where he was pointing. The floodlit ruins of the Parthenon up on the Acropolis. Athens' most famous landmark.

Solomon Daisy looked up at the Acropolis, then back at Dinu. 'Dinu Balan,' he said, 'you are smarter than you look.'

I couldn't decide whether to kiss Dinu or kick him, but it didn't matter. I was too busy trying not to be sick.

# 12
# Plan P for Parthenon

As we soon discovered, the problem with putting a time portal in Athens's most famous monument was that the Parthenon was guarded by night watchmen with dogs.

But guards could be bribed.

Solomon Daisy's wallet stuffed with euros and dollars soon meant that we were creeping across uneven rocks to the floodlit Parthenon, the temple gleaming white against the black night sky.

'I thought of this place first,' wheezed Solomon Daisy, stopping to rest his hands on his knees, 'but it's so high-profile. Also,' he gasped, 'it's so high.'

We were going up the less-well-known route past the Theatre of Dionysus, in the hope that it wouldn't be as well guarded as the famous touristy entrance. We had just passed the site of the Temple to Asclepius when Geoff with a G hissed, 'Guard! Get down!'

All five of us hit the stony ground and froze.

'I don't see a guard,' whispered Dinu a moment later.

'I'm sure I heard footsteps behind us,' hissed Geoff.

'Just your imagination,' muttered Jeff with a J.

He slowly stood up to a half-crouch and then beckoned us on. I felt as if I was in a black ops simulation game.

Even though it was a side route, it still took us through the Propylaea, the monumental entrance to the Acropolis. It was inky black in there, and a relief to emerge into the main sanctuary.

The Parthenon rose up on our right, lit by dazzling floodlights at its base.

'We have to go round to the far side, right?' said Dinu.

'Correct,' said Jeff with a J.

We were now close enough to see scaffolding, cranes and even some metal train tracks, presumably for carting huge blocks of Pentelic marble back and forth. They were obviously repairing the temple.

I don't quite know how we did it: a fat man, two skinny nerds with backpacks and two schoolboys sneaking up the Acropolis to the Parthenon and then around to its eastern entrance and finally up the giant floodlit steps, all without being spotted. But we managed.

I had been here a few years ago with my gran, before they roped it off for repairs. I'd forgotten how massive the columns were. Inside, they cast a good shadow for us to hide in.

'OK, Jeff and Geoff,' wheezed Solomon Daisy. He was still breathing hard from the climb. 'Figure out where to set it up and let's do this.' He glanced at his watch. 'It's almost two in the morning.'

Jeff looked around. 'When we were originally thinking of putting the portal here, I figured out where the cult statue of Athena would be.' He pointed. 'See? That would have been the base. The ancient geographer Pausanias tells us that the temple was full of tributes and gifts. It would have been like a museum storehouse. Probably the only empty space would have been right in front of the statue.'

'Wait!' I said. 'Didn't the statue of Athena stand out there?' I pointed outside, between two massive columns.

Before Solomon Daisy could reply, Dinu said, 'There was another statue of her inside the temple. Made of ivory and gold. There was a shallow pool of water in front of it to keep the ivory from cracking. We can land there.'

We all stared at him.

'You're right,' said Cool Jeff. 'But how on earth . . . ?'

'*Ancient Greek Assassins*,' said Dinu smugly.

'Of course,' I said.

'Bravo!' Solomon Daisy's glasses glinted in the floodlights. 'Ready to do this?'

Dinu and I looked at each other. I felt sick. This time I knew what I was in for. But the rewards would be awesome. Dinu mouthed the words, 'Fame and fortune.' We understood each other perfectly.

So we both nodded.

'Good!' said Solomon Daisy. 'Guys, set it up as quickly as you can.'

Jeff with a J unslung his backpack. 'The day and year are already programmed in,' he said. 'All we need to do is open it up and turn it on.'

The two of them pulled tubes out of their shoulder bags and started assembling the portal.

Solomon Daisy looked at us. 'A good mentor always gives the heroes a talisman before he sends them on a quest. But as you can't take anything, I'm giving you a phrase. A mantra. You might even call it a "talismantra".' He took a deep breath and spoke in ancient Greek: 'We seek Socrates, the lover of wisdom, the wisest man in Athens.'

Dinu and I dutifully recited the Greek phrase three times: 'We seek Socrates, the lover of wisdom, the wisest man in Athens.'

'Good,' said Daisy. 'That talismantra will keep your minds focused on the quest and help you achieve your goal.'

'I think I might need to vomit,' I said, and hurried towards one of the massive columns. Then I saw something that made me forget to be sick: two dark shapes coming up the rocky slope, right towards the temple. They were guards.

And that wasn't the worst thing.

'Guards are coming!' I gasped a few moments later. 'And they've got a dog with them!'

'Guys!' said Solomon Daisy. 'Is it ready?'

'Yes, boss!' said Jeff with a J.

'We're as ready as we'll ever be,' said Geoff with a G.

In the time it had taken me to go to the column and back, Geoff and Jeff had set up the portal and were standing either side of it with their Xbox controllers.

There it was: a big flat hoop shimmering with fire. The first time I had gone through, the flames had been a golden orange colour. Now they were a spooky lavender with blue sparks, like a gas fire.

I didn't have time to ask why the colour of the portal was different.

'Strip off your clothes and go!' commanded Solomon Daisy. 'All you have to do to get ten mil and a starring role in *Back to Athens* is spend a little time with Socrates and then tell me what he was really like.'

From outside the temple I heard Greek voices shouting and a dog barking.

Dinu was already half undressed so I stripped off too. I looked up just in time to see Dinu step boldly through the shimmering purple portal. For a moment it flashed blue, then it shimmered again.

A shrill whistle pierced the night.

'Stop!' called a voice in Greek. 'Stop right now!'

'Stop or we'll set the dog on you!' called the second voice, in accented English.

I looked at Solomon Daisy. What if the guards arrested him and his two tech guys? What if the dogs savaged them? Then we'd never get back!

Daisy grinned at me and fanned his sweating face with a dozen five-hundred-euro bills. 'Don't worry about us. We'll be fine! Guards can be bribed. Now GO!'

With trembling hands I tugged off my underpants, took three shaky steps forward, offered up a silent prayer and stepped through the portal.

# 13

# **Wet Landing**

Going back in time the first time had been horrible. Going back this time was worse. It was almost as if we were doing something against nature.

Which of course we were.

I was prepared to suffer the fizzing cells but now there was an added element of heat. I felt like a ping-pong ball in an oven: hollow inside and baking outside. My skin wasn't just prickly; it felt as if it was on fire. Luckily Dinu had been right about the pool of water in the temple.

'Argh!' I rolled around in the shallow water and tried to muffle my screams in case any temple priests were nearby.

'Dude!' came Dinu's groan. 'Are you there?'

'Unggh!' I managed to grunt. The water was only about ankle-deep. I wallowed in it like a porpoise in a puddle.

But as soon as my skin was cool the wave of nausea swept

over me. Thankfully I was as empty as a black hole and had nothing to expel. Beside me, I was aware of Dinu retching too, but a night of vomiting followed by a two-day fast meant dry heaves.

Groaning softly, I sat up in the shallow pool and splashed water on my glued-together eyes. Finally I managed to prise them open.

The temple was lit a deep purple by the still glowing portal but with no blinding floodlights outside.

'I think we made it!' I whispered. 'It must be night here too, and the temple is closed.'

'Oh my God!' breathed Dinu. 'Look behind you and up.'

Still sitting naked in the shallow pool, I twisted around. Far above us, the purple light of the portal showed us the two-storey tall statue of the goddess of wisdom, weaving and warfare: Athena.

I felt a shiver go through me.

Now that my eyes were adjusting, I began to make out shapes in the darkness. I could see the golden folds of Athena's robes and her pale ivory arms. She held a figure about our size in her right hand and a massive shield rested against her left leg, which was slightly bent.

Here and there a few thin beams of moonlight shone through some small holes and cracks in the temple roof. The portal was still glowing lavender and the overall effect was like being on another planet.

'I think I see a lamp,' murmured Dinu. 'On the base of the statue. At the goddess's feet.'

There was the soft plop of water to my left as he got up.

I splashed my eyes again and saw a soft gold light floating towards me. Soaking-wet Dinu was holding a flickering oil lamp, and it made him look as shiny as a bronze statue of Apollo.

He held out his hand, and when I grabbed it he pulled me to my feet.

I looked down at the pool in which we were standing. It was as long and wide as a London bus, but the shallow water barely reached my ankles. The surface of the water was purple, but light from Dinu's oil lamp made the gilded tiles at the base of the pool glint.

'You were right about the pool,' I said.

He nodded and held up the oil lamp. 'Let's find some clothes. Remember Jeff said there would be all sorts of offerings either side of Athena?'

It was a hot night and apart from my feet I was already dry. Now I could smell burning olive oil in the lamp and from somewhere else a spicy incense that made me want to sneeze.

The ancient geographer Pausanias had been right. The space either side of the cult statue was crowded with objects. I followed Dinu, open-mouthed, as the globe of yellow light from the oil lamp revealed statues large and small, bracelets, rings, earrings and necklaces, all arranged on beautiful tables and chests. There were also dozens of black-and-red vases like ones I'd seen in museums. Plus tripods: those shallow bronze bowls on three tall bronze legs that look like ancient barbecues.

'It's like Aladdin's cave!' he breathed.

'But we're not here for treasure,' I reminded him. 'We're here to find something to wear!'

# 14
# Getting Dressed

Dinu and I moved among the treasures in the Temple of Athena, looking for clothes.

After only a few minutes he set the lamp down on a small marble-topped table and picked up something like a crinkly sleeveless T-shirt. '*Eureka!*' he cried and then, 'Wait – is this for girls or boys?'

'I think it's called a chiton,' I said. 'Boys wore them.'

He gave it a sniff, nodded happily and pulled it over his head.

'What about me?' I said. 'Do you see anything there for me?'

'Here.' He reached into the gloom and handed me a similar one, only longer.

'I think this is a girl's dress,' I muttered. 'But I'll put it on until we find something better.'

I pulled it over my head.

Every Easter my gran makes a special meal and tells me to get out 'the linen tablecloth'. It belonged to her Greek great-grandmother and was woven on a loom. Linen has a particular feel between your finger and thumb, a certain texture to the weave. When I slipped on the dress in the Parthenon I knew immediately it was also linen.

It felt nice against my skin: light and cool. But it dragged on the polished marble floor.

'See any belts?'

'Try this.'

I tied the cord around my waist and then pulled up some of the fabric so that it bloused around the belt and exposed my feet and ankles.

'That's better,' I murmured. 'Have you got one?'

'Yes. I found a nice leather one with a dagger in a scabbard.'

'Hey! No fair! I'm dressed like a girl and you get a tunic and dagger.'

'Here.' Dinu passed me a sword.

'This is way too heavy. And I have nowhere to put it.'

'Then find your own dagger.'

I put down the sword and peered into the jumble of objects lit by flickering lamplight.

Then I spotted some fancy sandals made of gilded leather. They were just my size so I slipped them on.

Deeper among the maze of treasures I found a small iron dagger with an ivory handle in a woven sheath. I stuck it in my cord belt. I also grabbed a pearl-and-emerald necklace that might come in handy. I reckoned I could sell off the jewels one by one. The easiest way to carry it was to wear it, so I slipped it over my head.

I felt a pang of guilt and looked up at Athena, still glowing in the pulsing ultraviolet light of the portal.

I had a strange mental image of her slowly turning her head to look down at us with those frighteningly realistic eyes.

'Dinu,' I whispered, as if her ivory ears might be able to hear me, 'do you think it's bad luck to take things offered to the goddess?'

'It's fine. She's not real.'

'I hope you're right.' I shuddered. 'The last thing we want to do is anger any supernatural powers.'

At that moment a flash of blue illuminated the inside of the temple and we heard a splash and a groan.

'Oh no!' hissed Dinu. 'I think someone else has come through the portal!'

## 15

# Party Crasher

'**B**low out the lamp!' I hissed. 'Don't make a noise!'

Dinu blew out the flickering flame of the oil lamp and for a moment the world was black.

Then a familiar girl's voice groaned in the darkness. 'Dinu! Alex! Help!'

'Onions!' Dinu used one of his favourite Romanian swear words. 'It's my sister!'

I realised I had been holding my breath. 'Your *sister*?'

'Yeah.' Then he called out, 'Stay there, Crina! We're coming!'

We groped our way back through the tripods, tables and vases until we reached the reflecting pool at the foot of the cult statue.

The portal was no longer glowing, but a single oil lamp still burned at the goddess's feet. It dimly showed the shape of someone sitting in the water.

'Crina, is that you?' whispered Dinu.

'Dinu!' she cried. 'Where are you?'

'Right here.' He splashed through the pool and helped her up.

'Oh, Dinu!' She threw her arms around her brother. 'Going through the portal was horrible.'

The flickering oil-light at the base of the statue was just bright enough to show Crina in a wet dress plastered to her body. It looked like the turquoise one she had worn at dinner the first night.

'Crina!' I cried. 'You're wearing clothes! You're supposed to come through naked!'

'Yeah. Like that was ever going to happen!' she groaned.

'Why didn't her clothes burn?' Dinu asked me.

'Maybe because she landed in water?'

'My dress is linen,' said Crina. 'It's one-hundred-per-cent-organic. Made of a pounded plant called flax.' Suddenly she bent forward as if she had stomach cramps. 'Oh, I feel sick.'

'It will pass,' I said. I squinted in the darkness and saw that her hair was plaited and pinned up in an ancient hairstyle.

'Crina,' I said, 'are you wearing any metal hairpins?'

'Of course not,' she said. 'They're wood and bone. Organic. And I don't have any metal fillings in my teeth.'

'How did you know that metal fillings could explode but that organic material might not burn?'

There was a pause. Then, 'From your diary.'

'What diary?' I said, but I had a terrible feeling I knew.

'The one you wrote about your trip to Roman London.'

Dinu turned on me. 'You wrote a diary about our trip? You weren't supposed to say anything.'

'I didn't *say* anything,' I protested. 'But I did *write* some stuff down.' I rounded on Crina. 'You went through my things?'

'Just a little. That time I came round to get Dinu and the two of you were still up on the common? You really shouldn't leave private things lying around.'

'It wasn't lying around!' I spluttered. 'It was on my desk, in my room, hidden under some old school notebooks.'

'Yeah. I asked your gran if I could use the loo, but your bedroom door was open and I couldn't resist looking around. The first few pages were really good so I snuck it home to read it.'

'You actually took it *home*? That's stealing!'

'You write really well,' she said.

'Really?' I felt a flush of pleasure warm my cheeks.

'Yeah. I thought it was fiction at first. Then I googled Solomon Daisy and realised he was real. When you won that free holiday to Athens I figured he was behind it.'

'You what?'

'Sure. It was obvious.'

Dinu shook his head. 'She figured it out before we did, dude.'

I saw her eyes gleam in the moonlight as they grew wider. 'You *didn't* know he was planning to send you back? I thought you knew and were ignoring our deal.'

'What deal?'

'You promised that if you ever went back, you'd take me with you.'

'I swear we had no idea what he was plotting until yesterday morning when he turned up in his limo.'

Dinu said, 'How did you know to come through the portal here and now?'

'At the hotel, I used a glass pressed against the wall to eavesdrop, like before. I heard you talking about being picked up tonight at eleven thirty. So I put on black jeans and a black hoodie over my Greek-style dress. Then I snuck down early, around eleven fifteen. I hailed a taxi and got him to wait across the street. When you guys left, I followed you to the first place and then here to the Parthenon . . .'

'I knew somebody was following us!' said Dinu.

'Then,' said Crina, 'I watched you go through.'

I flushed. 'So you saw me . . . ?'

'Yeah. I saw you naked. No biggie. Anyway, when the guards were talking to Solomon Daisy and the tech guys, I took off my jeans and hoodie and ran through after you.'

Dinu started speaking in urgent Romanian.

She interrupted him in English. 'No way am I staying here until the portal comes on again! And I'm not going straight back either. I'm better prepared for this than you are.'

She took a step towards the edge of the pool but her knees wobbled and if we hadn't jumped forward to catch her, she would have fallen back in the water. When I put my arm around her, to help her out, I could feel her shivering.

I almost felt sorry for her but then she giggled. 'What are you wearing, Alex? You're dressed like a girl.'

I took my arm from around her shoulders. 'This place isn't exactly TK Maxx,' I snapped. 'This was all I could find.'

'*So what is plan?*' she said.

In Greek.

Once again, I was impressed.

'You've been learning Greek?'

'*Panu gay,*' she said. Certainly. 'I can say "Hello", "I'm lost" and "I would like . . ."'

'That last one is modern Greek,' I said.

'*Alay-thay leg-ace, O Soak-rah-tace,*' she said. You speak the truth, Socrates.

I couldn't help grinning, but Dinu was not so easily charmed. He folded his arms across his chest. 'The plan is to find Socrates and then come straight back here in twenty-four hours. For that, Alex and I get ten mil each.'

'I can help.'

'You're not getting a penny of my money,' he said.

'I don't care about your stupid money. I want to see what ancient Athens looks like.' She turned to me. 'You promised

68

I could come with you.'

I said, 'You can come with us on one condition. Promise to stay close and not talk. Right, Dinu?'

'Right.' I could hear the grin in his voice. 'You have to be like our slave.'

A noise near the front of the temple made us all turn.

'What was that?' hissed Dinu.

'I don't know,' I said. 'We'd better get out of sight.'

But it was too late. The massive double doors of the temple swung open to show a bearded man with a brightly flaming torch.

He was flanked by two archers wearing something like striped pyjamas and Smurf hats. They looked utterly bizarre.

But I didn't laugh.

They already had their arrows notched and pointed at us.

# 16
# **Threshold Guardians**

Most languages have a singular and a plural. Singular is the form a word takes when there is only one.

You, for example.

As in, 'I am pointing an arrow at you' when there is only one of you.

Plural is for more than one.

As in, 'We are pointing arrows at you' when there are lots of you.

But ancient Greek has something called a 'dual' which they use for just two things, especially a pair:

As in, *a pair of oxen, a pair of hands, a pair of ears . . .*

So when the man with the beard shouted 'Don't move or we'll shoot the two of you!' using the dual form of 'you', I was confused at first.

Then I realised what it meant.

He hadn't seen Crina.

She must have slipped into the shadows.

As Dinu and I put up our hands like in the movies, I hissed, 'Don't look for Crina! They haven't spotted her.'

He gave a small nod and kept his eyes front.

The archers came forward and grabbed us roughly by an arm each. They smelled so strongly of sweat and urine that I wondered if they ever bathed. The two of them shoved us, over the threshold of the temple and down three massive stairs. Once outside the sacred precinct of the temple, they forced us down on our knees at the feet of Beardy Guy, who wore a long robe and fancy sandals. The stony ground was just as hard back then as it was in our time.

'Who are you two?' demanded Beardy Guy, who I reckoned had to be a priest. 'What were you doing in the Temple of the Maiden at this hour?'

His accent was bizarre, nothing like what they'd taught us at the Living Greek School, but I could understand him enough to know he was still using the dual form.

'Please, sir,' I said, 'we are travellers from a faraway land. We were seeking refuge in the Temple of the Maiden.'

'They are obviously runaway xlave,' said one of the Smurf-hatted guards. His accent was even stranger than the priest's. He left off the last consonant of some words and used an X sound instead of an S.

'We are not slaves!' I protested. 'We are . . .' I managed to remember the word: 'freeborn!'

'Even if you're not slaves,' said the priest, reaching down to grasp my emerald-and-pearl necklace, 'you are thieves! I recognise this as a recent tribute to the Maiden.'

'I knew it was a bad idea to take offerings to the goddess,' I muttered in English.

'Maybe this whole trip was a bad idea,' groaned Dinu.

'Quiet!' commanded the priest. 'Do not profane the sacred precinct with your barbarian babbling!' He turned to the archers. 'Strip them and take them to prison. I will inform the council in the morning.'

'No!' I cried. I clung to his knees in the time-honoured fashion of the conquered to the conqueror. 'Please, sir. We were robbed. Have mercy on us.'

I glanced up but his face was as hard as granite.

We had to strip.

Although it was a warm night, we stood shivering as the priest took our clothes and headed back into the temple.

'I hope he doesn't catch Crina,' I said.

'She may be a pain,' said Dinu, 'but she's sensible. She'll stay hidden until the portal comes on tomorrow night. I'm more worried about us.'

'I know,' I whispered. 'I wonder what they do to temple thieves?'

As I looked around for a means of possible escape, moonlight showed the famous smaller temple called the Erechtheum. Its columns were shaped like women and they seemed to stare at me accusingly.

'Who are these Smurf guys, anyway?' muttered Dinu as they set about tying our wrists behind us. 'They stink.'

'I think they're Scythian archers. The ancient Athenians used them as a police force.'

'I don't remember that from *Ancient Greek Assassins*,' he said.

After our wrists were bound, the two smelly archers marched us away from the Parthenon. They had no torches, but the moon was bright enough for me to see a forest of bronze statues.

Then I caught sight of the biggest one of all and for a moment I almost forgot to be afraid. The colossal bronze statue of Athena stood with her back to us, as tall as a cathedral. She held a spear in her right hand and a massive shield leaned against her left leg. The moonlight painted her silver and black.

As her lofty face came into view I felt a shiver go through me, and not just because I was naked, bound and barefoot.

'Wow!' I breathed, looking up. And then, 'Ow!' as one of the smelly Scythians shoved me forward.

But I couldn't keep my eyes off the massive statue of Athena with a bazillion stars blazing above her head. I turned and sank to my knees before her.

'Forgive us, Athena,' I prayed loudly in ancient Greek, hoping to soften the Scythians' hearts. 'We were going to return your gifts to you. We were only borrowing them.'

'Quiet!' growled one of the archers. He tugged me roughly to my feet and then shoved me towards the Propylaea, the giant gateway of the Acropolis.

'I think I'm going to be sick,' whispered Dinu, as we plunged into the black shadows of the marble gateway. 'What should we do?'

'In situations like this,' I said, 'there's only one thing to do – pray!'

'Was our God around back then?' he asked.

'Of course, you fool. God is eternal.'

So we both prayed under our breath, him in Romanian and me in English. We prayed to God and Jesus Christ and Mary and even Saint Nektarios, patron saint of bees.

As we came out of the inky shadows cast by the gatehouse roof, I prayed again to Athena. 'Dear Athena,' I said out loud in ancient Greek, 'please save us and help us find Socrates.'

At this, Archer One grabbed my arm and turned me to face him. 'Xocrate?' he said. 'You want Xocrate?'

'Yes!' I said eagerly. Then I recited: 'We seek Socrates, the lover of wisdom, the wisest man in Athens!'

I saw the two Scythians exchange surprised glances.

Was it possible our talismantra might actually work?

# 17

# Ways to Die in Athens

Our talismantra did not save us.

Although Archer One did raise his eyebrows in a questioning look, Archer Two scowled and tipped his head back for a 'no'.

They pushed us on again and I almost tumbled down the monumental stairway that tourists would use two and a half thousand years later.

My heart was still thudding hard as we passed the small Temple of Athena Nike on our left, and we caught our first glimpse of ancient Athens below us. My gran and I have spent the last few summers in Greece at my aunt's seaside apartment and I'd been into the centre of Athens a couple of times. But what I'd seen then looked nothing like the ancient city.

In the moonlight it seemed hardly bigger than a village. The scattered houses looked like little white Lego bricks with red tile roofs. Although it was night, it was warm and I could hear the rhythmic creaking of cicadas, those tiny little cricket things that sit on tree branches and make up for their invisibility by filling the world with their noise.

Could this sleepy village really be the home of some of the greatest minds who had ever lived? Playwrights like Euripides, Sophocles, Aeschylus and Aristophanes? The father of history, Herodotus, and his brilliant successor, Thucydides? Beautiful and clever women like Aspasia? And of course the philosophers, the men who first examined the meaning of life? Could they really be found in this moonlit village?

When we finally reached the foot of the Acropolis stairs, the smelly Smurf guards prodded us to the right.

They made us hurry along a road of hard-packed earth flanked by two-storey buildings I took for houses. Up close the sleeping houses presented blank plaster walls with only a few high slits for windows. Where the plaster was coming off, I could see mud brick underneath.

We were barefoot and I tried not to yelp every time my tender sole landed on a shard of clay or a piece of grit. But then I stepped in something squishy and smelly. My worst fears were confirmed as I caught a whiff of dog poo.

'Dude, you stepped in it!' groaned Dinu.

'That's the least of our problems,' I muttered. 'They're

taking us to prison, and I just remembered what they do to criminals.'

'What?'

'The worst ones include nailing you to a plank alive–'

'Oh my God!' groaned Dinu.

'– or they make you drink a kind of poison called hemlock. That's how they executed Socrates.'

We came to a crossroads with a giant fig tree, where we could go north, south, east or west. Our guards prodded us north along the dirt road and my stomach flipped as we approached a high, stone-walled building up ahead on the right. Was it the prison?

No.

We passed it. From within its walls, I heard the faint sound of a flute and tambourine. It sounded spooky on this deserted, moonlit night.

'Aghh!' I cried at the sudden sight of a pale man standing stock still up ahead.

But it wasn't a man. It was a painted marble head of a man on a square column. His eyes and beard were painted black and he wore a strange frozen smile. In place of arms he had two square stubs with garlands hanging from them.

'Dude, what's that?' hissed Dinu.

'I think it's called a herm,' I whispered back. 'After the god Hermes. They guard crossroads, doorways and boundaries against evil spirits.'

'Creepy,' said Dinu.

'Quiet!' snapped one of the Scythians.

But as we passed it, both our guards reached out to touch the herm's chin behind his short painted beard, presumably for good luck.

I spotted a slab of marble on the other side of the road. It had letters carved into it, a Greek inscription. There were no spaces between the letters but they had been filled in with dark paint and I managed to read it:

IAMTHEBOUNDARYOFTHEAGORA

'I am the boundary of the Agora,' I murmured.

'What?' said Dinu miserably.

'We must be coming into the Agora. The ancient marketplace. The place where Socrates liked to hang out. So near and yet so far,' I added. That was something my dad used to say.

'Wait!' hissed Dinu. 'Didn't they put Socrates in prison for a whole month before he had to drink hemlock? Maybe he'll be in the prison. Maybe he can help us escape. If he's the wisest man in the world . . .'

For a moment my spirits lifted. Then I did the maths.

'Nice idea, but I think his prison was near the Acropolis. And Socrates won't be arrested until at least another ten or twelve years in the future.'

'The future,' said Dinu with a bitter laugh.

'Yeah,' I muttered as one of the guards shoved me forward, 'I don't see us having much of a future now.'

# 18
# Golden Boy

A few steps into the Agora our guards steered us to the left so that we were now walking past a stoa, a covered walkway where people could take refuge from the heat of the day. I had visited a reconstructed stoa in Athens the year before. This one was longer, thinner and shabbier.

On our right was a massive dirt field dotted with shrines and statues: the Market Square. A broad road flanked by plane trees cut across it. The trees, shrines and statues all cast inky-black shadows in the moonlight.

It seemed to me there were plenty of places to hide. I was wondering how far I would get if I made a break for it when the sound of strange buzzy music behind us made our guards stop and turn.

The golden glow of torchlight trembled on the ground and a moment later a procession came into the Agora after us.

There were ten of them.

Girls and boys in their teens and twenties. Not much older than me and Dinu. Only two of them looked over thirty.

In the lead were two pretty flute-girls with crinkly dresses, fringed shawls and pinned-up hair wrapped in cloth bands. Then came two boys in short chitons, followed by four young men in short cloaks over chitons. Taking up the rear were two older men. They had short beards and flowered garlands but no chitons, only blanket-like cloaks. One of the men was short and stocky, with curly dark hair. The other was tall, blond and muscular. When they saw us they stopped playing music, held up their torches and stared at us open-mouthed.

I suppose we must have looked pretty strange: two butt-naked boys standing in the flickering torchlight, guarded by two stripy archers.

Holding out his torch, the blond guy came closer with his head cocked to one side. He was obviously the leader, for the others followed. Up close, I could see he was movie-star handsome. He wore some kind of purple cloak like Jay-Z might wear a Superman cape, letting it drag on the ground. His skin was tanned, his body ripped and the yellow torchlight made the hair beneath his garland shine like gold.

'My dear Scythians!' He took another step forward, staggered and managed not to fall. 'Where are you taking these beautiful boys?' He was obviously drunk and this gave him a strange way of speaking, mixing up his Ls and his Rs. 'They're delightful!'

'General!' stammered Scythian Number One. 'These are runaway xlave and thieve.' He was gazing at the blond guy just like I would stare if the actor who plays Thor walked into our local Tesco.

'We are taking them to the Xtate Prison,' added Scythian Number Two. He also seemed star-struck.

The Scythian had pronounced the man's name strangely: Al-kib-YAH-day. But suddenly I realised who he was. I looked at Dinu and we both said together: 'It's Alcibiades!'

'From *Ancient Greek Assassins*!' confirmed Dinu.

'And also from Plato,' I said. 'This guy was a friend of Socrates! Remember the excerpt from the dialogue we studied in Rome? This could be our chance to escape!'

I needed to think of a clever ruse.

But Alcibiades got there first.

'Why, those are *my* slaves!' he slurred. 'Thank you for bringing them back to me!'

The first Scythian frowned. 'How can that be, xir? We caught them in the Temple of the Maiden. They were wearing clothing, jewellery and weapon pillaged from Athena.'

For a moment Alcibiades just swayed gently with his head still cocked to one side. Then he laughed.

'Of course you did!' He gestured vaguely with the flaming

torch. 'It was a challenge I set them. They were going to bring some treasures to me as proof of their loyalty, and then return them in the morning.' He winked at Dinu and said, 'Right, boys?'

Dinu looked blank – maybe the Greek was too advanced for him – but I played along: 'Yes, master! We did just as you said.'

I nudged Dinu and he echoed me: 'Yes, master!'

'Boy! Give me silver!' lisped Alcibiades. Without turning, he clicked his fingers impatiently.

'Yes, master.' Like a magician, one of the boys stuck his forefinger in his mouth, pulled out two silver coins and handed them over. I guessed he was a slave.

'Here!' Alcibiades staggered forward and handed a shiny wet coin to each of the Scythians. 'I will speak to the priest in the morning and sort everything out.'

The Scythians looked at each other and then at the coins in their hands. Then they shrugged, grinned and each put his coin in his own mouth, between gum and cheek.

And then – St Nektarios be praised! – they cut us free.

A moment later they had disappeared into the inky shadows.

'Girls!' cried Alcibiades in his strange slurred baby talk. 'Lend these two your shawls. We're not in the palaestra.'

Giggling, the two pretty flute-girls pulled the fringed shawls from around their shoulders and handed them to us. Dinu got the green one and I got pink. I was about to protest about getting the girly colour, but then I shut up. Anything was better than being naked.

The flute-girls played a jaunty tune as we started to tie the shawls around our waists.

'Girls, help them out!' laughed Alcibiades.

Giggling, the girls showed us how to wrap the shawls. Like a bath towel when you've just come out of the shower, only with one end over our left shoulders.

Alcibiades leaned forward, his head still tipped to one side.

'Now,' he said, pushing his garland up out of his eyes, 'who are you and what are your names?'

'I'm Alexis and this is Dinu, short for Dionysius,' I stammered. We had previously agreed to use popular personal names close to our own, which were of Greek origin anyway.

'I'm Alcibiades, as you know, and this is my friend Antiochus the famous admiral. Tell me, Alexis and Dinu: are you really runaway slaves?'

'No, sir,' I said. 'We seek Socrates, the lover of wisdom, the wisest man in Athens.'

'Socrates,' echoed Dinu.

'Ah, Socrates!' Alcibiades stood up and slapped his thighs and turned away in mock distress. 'The bane of my life!'

He didn't seem drunk now.

'We would very much like to meet him,' I said. Then I added, 'Also, we left Dinu's sister Crina in the temple of

Athena on the Parthenon. We need to let her know we're all right and to stay put and wait for us.'

'We shall do both!' The general clapped his hands together and then lisped, 'Presently I will send one of my slaves to fetch your sister. And together we will try to find Socrates. But just now we're off to a special ceremony of death and rebirth. Come!'

*Death and rebirth?*

Dinu and I exchanged a quick look of alarm. And even though it was a warm night, I shuddered.

## 19
# Gong Bath

Landing in the past at night made ancient Athens seem even stranger and more dreamlike.

The flute-girls led the way down the broad tree-lined road I had first spotted when we came into the Agora. It was now at least two hours after midnight and the full moon splashed inky-black shadows onto the road.

I knew from *Athens on Five Drachmas a Day* that this must be the Panathenaic Way, a famous road that led from the Acropolis to the Dipylon Gate. Sometimes there were chariot races here and religious processions involving almost the whole population.

But tonight there seemed to be nobody else alive in the world, just our strange little jingly, jangly torchlit procession.

After a while we turned off to the right and Alcibiades banged on the double doors of a two-storey house with a herm outside. Almost immediately the doors swung open and we passed into a torchlit courtyard.

A stocky man with a grey beard and a younger round-faced guy with hardly any beard came to greet us. Both of them were wearing long chitons rather than blanket-cloaks.

'Are these the initiates?' Greybeard frowned at us. 'I thought you were bringing four, not six.'

Alcibiades nodded at me and Dinu. 'These two are sent by the goddess.'

'Surely they are too young?'

'And yet I came upon them in the Agora, naked and godlike in their beauty.' He turned his head and murmured something into the older man's ear.

Greybeard nodded. 'Then they are obviously meant to participate. You did well. Are you still willing to lead the ceremony?'

'I am,' said Alcibiades.

'Good.' He turned to us. 'Once you are clean, you may come into the *andron*.'

A slave in a knee-length tunic and with shoulder-length hair came over to us with a pitcher, basin and a linen cloth draped over his arm.

When he had washed our feet – I felt a bit bad for him, but it was a relief to be rid of the dog poo between my toes – he showed us into a banqueting room lit by hanging oil lamps.

There were deer skins on the floor, dark-red walls and six dining couches, three on either side of the room right up against the walls.

At the far end a bronze tripod stood beside a wooden table. On the table were a jug, a deep type of cup that I knew was called a skyphos, and a whip.

Alcibiades, now dressed in a long white chiton, took up position between the table and the tripod.

Greybeard took the silver pitcher from the table and began pouring something into the skyphos, held by Round Face.

'Does this remind you of anything?' I whispered to Dinu in English.

'The Mithraeum ceremony?' came his almost silent reply.

'Exactly!' I said. 'It must be some kind of initiation.'

Then Alcibiades took the whip from the table. It had a plaited leather handle and three long leather straps.

I suddenly remembered how the priest of Mithras had pretended to attack initiates with a bow and arrows, and a sword.

Dinu had a queasy expression on his face. 'What's the horsewhip for, dude?'

'No idea.'

Alcibiades slowly lifted the whip. But instead of calling one of us forward for a beating, he used the handle to strike the rim of the tripod's bronze bowl.

A deep tone filled the room.

It wasn't a tripod. It was a gong. Or maybe it was a tripod *and* a gong.

Round Face was taking round the skyphos, making us all drink from it.

Was it hemlock?

When he brought it to me, I hesitated: the combination of gong noise and pine-smoke from the torches was making me dizzy.

'Don't worry,' said Round Face. 'It won't hurt you.'

I didn't want to argue. Instead I touched the cup to my lips and pretended to take a sip. It smelled like barley water with honey. And something bitter.

'What is it?' I asked.

The gong was still sounding, rising and falling. Its sound made every cell in my body vibrate.

'It's called *kykeon*,' said the man. 'The barley reminds us that we partake of the goddess Demeter and the honey is as sweet as Persephone.'

'There's something bitter too,' I said.

'That is a special herb. It will help you see the goddess.' He swirled the liquid in the goblet and took it to Dinu.

One of the young men who had already drunk from the cup suddenly swayed and steadied himself against a couch.

This distraction gave Dinu the chance to also pretend to drink.

Alcibiades was still making the gong hum. Even though

I hadn't drunk any of the potion, the sound seemed to change colour. Its deep vibration seemed purple-brown, then changed tone to become the colour of pale wheat, then green and finally blue. My mind went still. I could no longer tell where my body ended and the sound began. My gran sometimes does something called a gong bath at a yoga studio in Camberwell. Now I totally got it.

With no warning, Greybeard doused his torch. At first I saw only darkness. Presently my eyes adjusted to see that it wasn't totally dark. Seven little oil lamps were still burning and their light seemed to rise to the heavens.

They were bright enough for me to see smoke rising from the extinguished torch like a joss stick when the flame goes out. I was hypnotised by the pine-scented ribbon of smoke twisting up to the ceiling.

The smell and the deep humming of the gong was making me dizzy, so I stretched out on the nearest couch.

'Move over.' Dinu lay down beside me. 'This is amazing,' he murmured. 'Better than church.'

He was right. It was amazing. Part of me seemed to float up out of my body along with the lights.

I was actually looking down at myself, lying next to Dinu on a Greek banqueting couch.

I remembered the strange ceremony we had witnessed in Roman London, and my revelation that it was a way for the soul to know where to go once it left the body.

Was this the same sort of thing?

Before I could decide, a velvet blackness embraced me.

Some time later, the crowing of a rooster brought me out of a deep sleep.

For one heartbeat I didn't know where I was.

Then I smelled the stale smoke from a pine-pitch torch and remembered. When I sat up, I got another shock: the room was empty.

Alcibiades was gone.

And what was even worse, so was Dinu.

# 20
# Bed and Breakfast

I blinked around the deserted banqueting room. Last night it had been a scented three-dimensional map of the infinite cosmos, with stars and moons and planets. Last night my soul had floated up out of my body.

Now it was just a room with six couches, a bronze tripod and the faint smell of incense.

I felt groggy and disoriented. Had it all been a dream? Was I really in ancient Athens? Was Crina all right? And where was Dinu?

Outside, the cock crowed again.

As I slid off my couch, the pink shawl almost slipped off. Clutching it around my waist, I hurried out of the stale dining room.

Relief washed over me along with the cool air of the courtyard. The milky-blue light of dawn showed me nine men sitting on two benches either side of a long table.

One of them was Dinu, his green shawl draped like a mantle around his shoulders.

'Alexis,' he called in Greek. 'Come. Eat. It's good.' He moved up the bench to make a space for me.

As I came closer, I caught the scent of fresh bread and tangy vinegar. The men were dipping hunks of bread into silver bowls and drinking from actual golden goblets.

I tied my pink shawl around my waist, so it wouldn't slip off, and sat beside Dinu. 'What are you doing?' I muttered in English. 'We're not supposed to eat!'

'I don't care,' he whispered back in English. 'I am starving. Besides, what's the worst that could happen?'

'We know exactly what will happen,' I muttered. 'And it *is* the worst.' But I gazed longingly at half a dozen big chunks of bread and a shallow silver bowl of what looked like wine. There was a silver platter with a few cubes of goat's cheese and some olive pits.

Alcibiades sat across the table from us. His blond hair was damp and bound in a blue headband instead of last night's garland. In the growing light I could see a few fine wrinkles at the corners of his eyes, which were bright blue. I guessed he was about thirty-five.

A slave brought me a surprisingly heavy gold goblet, full of diluted wine by the smell of it.

I hesitated.

Then I remembered that the Romans used to add wine to

water because it makes it safe to drink. Apparently the wine kills most bacteria. Though of course they didn't know that. All they knew was that drinking water on its own could make you sick or even kill you.

I was about to quench my thirst when Dinu muttered, 'They all poured out a little of their wine first; you probably should too.'

I dribbled a libation onto the packed earth of the courtyard and said in Greek, 'Thank you, Dionysus, for the wine.'

Greybeard, Round Face and Alcibiades all nodded approvingly, so I drank.

The wine was well-watered: tart and refreshing. It cleared my head but gave me a slight buzz as well.

The slave returned with a fresh platter of goat's cheese cubes and little black olives and set it before me.

My stomach growled.

I looked at all the men chewing their bread with obvious enjoyment.

'Come on,' I told myself. 'You can do it. You've fasted for more than three days before. Be strong!'

Alcibiades cocked his head and raised his eyebrows at me. 'Aren't you hungry?'

'No,' I lied, but my growling stomach told the truth.

'Breaking the fast is part of the initiation,' he lisped.

'It's true,' said Greybeard. 'Also, our custom in Hellas is to offer hospitality to strangers.'

It took me a moment to remember that 'Hellas' was the ancient Greek word for Greece.

'And if you refuse to eat,' continued Greybeard with a smile, 'I will be deeply offended.'

That was when I gave into temptation and broke the second rule of time travel: I tucked into the food.

# 21
# The Charioteer

The olives were small, black and bitter. The cheese smelled like a flock of goats. Bread dipped in vinegar was just a soggy version of salt-and-vinegar crisps.

It was the best breakfast I'd ever had.

My stomach gurgled with happiness and I felt my spirits lift.

What a wonderful thing food is!

A slave was taking away the empty platter when the double doors of the courtyard swung open and a strong whiff of horses was followed by one of Alcibiades' slaves leading in two horses yoked to a small, light chariot.

'Master,' he said to the general. 'Xanthus has gone to the Temple of the Maiden to make sure the girl named Crina waits there for you. He will stay and protect her. And here is your chariot, as requested.'

I offered up a silent prayer that Crina would be looked

after. And suddenly I realised how lucky we had been to be rescued by Alcibiades.

The horses were beautiful – a black and a white.

Alcibiades rose to his feet. He was still wearing the white, ankle-length chiton from the night before, but had tied a blue sash just below his chest.

Everyone else stood up too.

Alcibiades turned to the four young men who had completed the initiation.

'Go to your homes and bid your families farewell,' he told them. 'Then put on your armour and meet me in the Piraeus. I'm putting you under the command of the best captain in the fleet.'

The four young soldiers thanked him and left.

'Dear Poulytion,' said Alcibiades to Greybeard, 'do you by chance have any spare chitons these boys can borrow?'

'For you, anything.' Greybeard snapped his fingers and a slave appeared. 'Find chitons for these boys. Belts and sandals too. Get some from Myron's chest.'

A few minutes later Dinu and I were dressed in unbleached linen chitons, his slightly too small and mine a bit big. The belts were a clever design. Each was essentially a band of soft leather folded over and stitched but with spaces in the seam where you could store coins or other small objects. If you wore it with the seam against your body then only you could get at it, making it like an ancient money belt.

The sandals were basic but good quality and almost new.

'Come on, boys!' lisped Alcibiades. 'I'm going to take you to see something.'

I looked up eagerly. 'Is it Socrates?'

'Better than Socrates,' he said. 'But first, come and meet the horses.'

He went to the white horse first. 'This is Thumos,' he said, 'the noblest beast I have ever owned. Stroke him and speak softly to him and he will take you anywhere.'

I stroked the white horse's neck and felt the warm power quivering beneath my fingertips.

Alcibiades moved over to stand beside the black, who tossed his head as his master reached out to stroke him, then blew hot breath through flaring nostrils. 'Be careful of this one! I call him Eros, after a story Socrates once told me.'

'I like Eros.' Dinu came up and patted the black's flank. Then he yelped as the black kicked out, missing him by mere millimetres.

'I told you to be careful!' laughed Alcibiades. He stepped onto the small chariot, took the reins from his slave and tied them around his waist. 'Get in,' he commanded.

I hesitated. The chariot wasn't anything like the ones I'd seen in movies. It was made of wood and wicker with a webbed leather floor attached to a slender wooden shaft. Even the wheels were made of wood.

'Both of us?' I said. 'In there?'

'Of course! No. Don't try to hang on to the chariot; it's too low for you to grip and too fragile. Hold on to me.'

When we stepped up behind Alcibiades, the leather webbing sagged under our weight and the wicker frame creaked as it listed slightly to port, where Dinu stood. There was only just room for three pairs of feet on the small, bouncy platform. It was like standing in a basket on wheels.

As we took our places, the black horse lifted his tail and deposited three big greenish-brown presents.

Alcibiades laughed and repeated, 'Hold on to me!'

We each hooked an arm around his middle. Beneath the gauzy ankle-length chiton I could easily feel the muscles of his waist.

A slave helped turn the horses to face the open doors out to the street. Out in the road, I saw half a dozen chickens pecking in the dust. Finally, the slave handed his master a horsewhip. Although it was just like the one he had used the night before to strike the gong, Alcibiades wielded this horsewhip in a very different way.

He made it crack behind the heads of the two horses and at the same time he shouted, 'Fly!'

An instant later we exploded out into the street, making the chickens squawk and scatter.

# 22

# Down to Piraeus

As the chariot shot out of the courtyard, Dinu and I held on for dear life.

A sharp left onto the broad Panathenaic Way sent men scattering, just like the chickens had done a moment before. On almost every face I saw expressions of alarm quickly turn to delight as they saw who was driving.

'Alcibiades!' some of them cried. A few others called out witty remarks like, 'Where are you going in such a hurry? The races are next month, not today!' or 'Did someone catch you kissing his wife?'

The Acropolis was straight ahead and between the trunks of the plane trees on both sides I glimpsed the Agora. I saw the reed awnings of a hundred stalls and plumes of smoke from braziers and caught a sudden whiff of fish.

'Market day?' I shouted, to be heard above the thundering hoofs.

Alcibiades nodded, turning his head enough for me to see his grin.

'Do you think Socrates might be here in the Agora today?'

'I'm sure of it.' He touched Eros with the leather thongs of his whip to make him run faster.

Three veiled women squealed and jumped out of our way and a couple of dogs ran barking after us.

Alcibiades tugged the reins and we veered to the right. Our wheel nearly knocked down a herm and now we were speeding past a long stoa whose columns flashed by on my left. It was the stoa from the night before, where Alcibiades had rescued us from the Smurf guards.

This road wasn't tree-lined and up ahead on the right I spotted the red parasol-shaped roof of the Tholos, with its distinctive diamond-shaped roof tiles. But we took a sharp left before we reached it and then another right. Dinu was laughing and I had a big grin too.

'I guess you *can* ride chariots in the streets of Athens!' I said to Dinu.

Alcibiades slowed down to cross a short bridge over a large open drain running beside the road. I caught the sickly-sweet smell of sewage. A tall stone building loomed on our left.

'There's the State Prison, where you almost spent the night,' he called over his shoulder. 'And that's the Street of the Marble Workers.'

We continued straight on, but glancing left I saw a street

full of nearly naked stone-masons who were so dusty with white powder that they looked like ghosts. I could hear the tapping and clinking of metal on stone, but already we were past that street and heading towards the arch of a gate in the city wall.

Two Scythian guards in striped leggings cheerfully saluted us and let us go through.

As we passed under the stone arch of the city gate the sound of horses' hoofs filled my ears. Then we came out under a vast open sky. We were outside the city now.

'Please!' came voices to our left. Several beggars sat among the weeds beside the road. Two of them were naked and the rest wore no more than scraps of clothing. One of them had no legs and only one arm.

Alcibiades ignored the beggars and cracked his whip to make the horses run. As we picked up speed I saw roadside stalls selling good-luck charms, ceramic pots and small marble figurines. Soon we were moving so fast that the stalls were only a blur.

'Where are we going?' I shouted in his ear.

'You'll see!' cried Alcibiades.

We had left the beggars and stalls behind. Now we were fairly flying and every bump in the road sent us bouncing up and down. We clung to our fearless driver with eyes wide and hearts thumping.

At one point, some goats were crossing from one side of

the road to the other and they scattered before us, but the flock of sheep we met a few minutes later weren't as nimble.

The animals got confused and clogged up the road, forcing Alcibiades to pull hard on the reins. Infuriated by this delay, the black horse reared up, forcing the white one to rise up too.

'Restrain yourself, Eros!' laughed Alcibiades, and laid his whip gently but firmly on the stallion's rump.

Eros responded with a rebellious snort and pawed the dirt road with his front right hoof, while a wide-eyed old shepherd urged his flock across.

'Where are you taking us?' I asked again.

'To the Piraeus, of course! To see the fleet!'

I tried to tell him we wanted to see Socrates, not the fleet, but it was no use.

We were off again, speeding between painted tombs and pink-flowered oleander bushes. It was no later than seven in the morning, I guessed, and the air was as fresh as clear water.

I had been on the road to Piraeus several times, but it was always crowded with traffic and grey with fumes. To ride in a bouncing chariot with a floor like a mini-trampoline was both terrifying and wonderful. The wind ruffled our tunics and the scent of thyme filled our heads. Sometimes we saw carts or riders or pedestrians up ahead, but they always swerved or scattered to make way.

'Woohoo!' cried Dinu as we actually sent two men diving into the bushes at the edge of the road. 'It's just like *Ancient*

*Greek Assassins!*' He punched the air but almost fell off and had to grab on to our driver with a yelp.

Then we crested a rise in the road and our eyes were dazzled by a sparkling ribbon of sea on the horizon. Straight ahead we saw the buildings of three harbours gleaming in the early-morning sun and beyond them the masts of a hundred ships looked like a forest floating on that ribbon.

'How many ships?' I shouted to Alcibiades.

'Two hundred!' he cried happily. 'And I'm in command of them all!'

Dinu and I looked at each other.

Then Dinu echoed his last words. 'You're in command of them all?'

'Yes! The expedition was my idea, so the people voted me the command. We need all the men we can get,' he shouted, 'and you two will make perfect spear-bearers.'

I don't think Dinu understood, but I did.

Alcibiades wasn't giving us a tour of the area around Athens; he was drafting us into his army.

# 23

# The Wrong Kind
# of Chariot

When they made the movie *Ben Hur* they used the wrong kind of chariots.

Miss Forte in Latin club told us that racing chariots were basically baskets on wheels. As light and fast as possible.

Imagine hitching your skateboard to a couple of wild stallions.

That's what ancient chariot racing would have been like.

That's what we were riding in.

'I think he's kidnapping us!' I shouted at Dinu in English.

'What?'

'He wants to make us his spear-bearers!'

'Cool!'

'No, Dinu! Uncool! Deeply uncool! We have to jump off! But wait until he slows down a little more,' I added.

Alcibiades looked over his shoulder at me and laughed.

'You are as white as a maiden,' he said. 'Don't worry – the two of you don't have to come on the expedition. But I need to speak to the captain of the fleet and I wanted you to see our navy.'

'Dude, I think he was joking about us being spear-bearers,' I said to Dinu.

'Oh, too bad.'

Soon we met more traffic bringing goods from the port, and Alcibiades had to slow his team to a trot. Eros and Thumos were covered with foamy sweat and snorting through their noses.

Painted tombs began to appear beside the road but once we passed under the arch of the port wall, they were replaced with warehouses and fenced-off storage areas. I spotted barrels and crates and bales of cloth. Taverns and shops came next, and then a great stoa whose painted columns revealed glimpses of market stalls inside.

The clatter of the horses' hoofs on wooden planks marked our arrival at the docks. Ships crowded the water before us. Some had their sails unfurled enough to display devices on them: owls, horses, gorgon heads . . . and a cupid with a thunderbolt in his hand.

Alcibiades reined in the team and tossed the straps to a long-haired sailor who wore nothing but a loincloth and a grin.

As Dinu and I stepped back off the chariot and onto the dock our legs were trembling so much that we had to hang on to each other in order not to fall down.

Dozens of men surged forward to greet Alcibiades. Two of them had handfuls of straw, with which they set about wiping down Eros and Thumos.

They all looked at Alcibiades with open adoration.

And he fairly glowed with pleasure at the attention.

From somewhere came the smell of roasting fish. It was so delicious that my stomach rumbled, even though I had just eaten. A naked boy brought something like a fish kebab, steaming hot. Alcibiades devoured it and then opened his mouth like a baby bird so another sailor could direct a red jet from a wineskin into it. Wine dribbled from the corner of his mouth and when he wiped it away with the back of his hand, it left a streak on his dusty face.

I would have liked something to wash the dust from my mouth too, but Alcibiades seemed to have forgotten about us. Dinu tapped me on the shoulder and pointed. Nearby was a fountain: a bronze lion roaring a gush of water into a marble tank.

Dinu and I both splashed our dusty faces and tentatively put our mouths under the spout of water. Thankfully it tasted fresh and clean.

Alcibiades was still busy chatting with his fans, but we didn't mind; the whole Athenian fleet lay before us. Dinu stepped from a bench behind the fountain onto the rim of the tank itself. He reached down and gave me a hand up. From up here on the marble rim of the fountain we were high enough to see men swarming on the decks of the ships, making preparations for their great expedition.

Some men were mending sails or making ropes. Others were polishing their armour or sharpening swords. I realised you could tell the sailors from the soldiers because the soldiers wore something called an *exomis* – a chiton that fastened over just one shoulder – but the sailors were almost nude.

In *Ancient Greek Assassins*, the ships are big and sturdy, but these ones looked alarmingly small and flimsy. One of them was slightly fancier than the rest. It had a thunderbolt-holding-cupid on its limp sail. Eyes were painted on the pointed front of the prow to make it resemble a kind of sea creature. The eyes were the same blue as Alcibiades'.

'What's happening?' I asked a man who was dipping his bucket in the fountain. 'Why are there so many ships here?'

The man grinned at me and said something in an accent so heavy I couldn't make out a word.

At my blank look, a boy standing nearby said, 'It's our whole fleet. Nearly every ship we've got. The army is about to depart!'

I stared at the boy in dismay. Alcibiades had mentioned an expedition, but I hadn't understood what he meant until just now.

'What's the matter, dude?' whispered Dinu.

'The tech guys got it wrong,' I hissed. 'They've sent us back to a time when Athens was still at war with Sparta. And judging from the size of the fleet, things are desperate.'

'Cool!' grinned Dinu. 'Maybe we'll get a chance to kill some Spartans for real.'

'No, Dinu.' I groaned. 'Killing Spartans for real would not be cool at all.'

# 24
# The Boy at the Fountain

'Tell me more about the fleet?' I asked the boy by the fountain.

He was about nine or ten, dressed in a good-quality sky-blue chiton and with striking dark eyes beneath a wide forehead. He said something, but the crowds and splashing of the water made it hard for me to hear.

'What?' I cupped my hand behind my ear.

The boy stepped up onto the bench and then onto the edge of the fountain beside me. When he wobbled I grabbed his arm to steady him.

'Thanks,' he said, and shaded his eyes. 'This is good. You can see the decks from here. It's the fleet for Syracuse,' he explained. 'My brother says they'll probably sail tomorrow or the day after.'

Dinu said, 'Is Syracuse in Sparta?'

The boy's broad forehead crinkled in a frown. 'Nowhere

near. Anyway, we're at peace with Sparta. Nicias brokered a fifty-year truce with their king almost six years ago.'

That meant Jeff and Geoff hadn't got it wrong.

Athens *was* at peace.

So why the ginormous expedition?

Something was niggling at my brain, but then Dinu distracted me.

'That must be his ship,' he said in English. 'The one with Eros – the god of love – holding a thunderbolt.'

'Probably,' I said. 'But listen, Dinu, we have to get back to Athens. We have to find Socrates. And then get your sister and go back home.'

'What language are you speaking?' asked the boy beside me. His eyes were so dark they were almost black.

'Um, the language of the Tin Islands, our country far across the sea.'

'Did I hear you mention Socrates?'

'Yes.' I recited our talismantra: 'We seek Socrates, the lover of wisdom, the wisest man in Athens.'

The boy's dark eyes gleamed. 'I will take you to Socrates, who is indeed the wisest man in Athens. My brother Glaucon and I just came down to see the fleet. We're about to return to the city.'

The boy couldn't have been more than ten but already he spoke with the fluency of someone twice his age. I guessed he had a big brain behind that big forehead.

'My friend and I came here with Alcibiades,' I said. 'He's promised to take us to see Socrates.'

'Alcibiades is famous for breaking promises.' The boy lifted his chin. 'See?'

I looked and, sure enough, Alcibiades was heading off towards one of the ships with his arm around a muscular, nut-brown sailor.

'Dinu!' I said in Greek. 'This boy is offering us a lift back to Athens. Come on!'

Dinu shook his head and jumped off the fountain edge. 'I want to go with Alcibiades to see the ships,' he said.

I switched to English. 'But what about Socrates and Crina?'

'Crina will be fine. Why don't I meet you back in the city in a few hours, after you've found Socrates?'

'Wait! Where?' And to the boy beside me, 'Where's a good place to meet?'

'A shoemaker called Simon has a shop across the street from the Tholos at the entrance to the Agora,' said the boy. 'If we can't find Socrates in the Lyceum or one of the stoas, then he might be there.'

'Dinu!' I called. 'Did you get that?'

'Get what?'

I cupped my hands around my mouth and shouted, 'Meet me at the house of Simon the Cobbler at noon! It's just across from the Tholos – that round-roofed building we passed on the way here.'

'All right, Wimpy!' Dinu called over his shoulder. 'See you then.'

I watched long enough to see him catch up with Alcibiades. Then I clambered down from the fountain and helped the boy down too.

'Thank you,' he said. 'My name is Aristocles. And that's my brother Glaucon.'

'Where's your cart?' I asked, looking around.

'No cart.' The boy thoughtfully picked his nose. 'We came on foot.'

'I thought you offered me a lift back?' I said.

The boy examined the tip of his finger, then wiped it on his chiton. 'No. I just said we'd take you to Socrates. I like listening to him too.'

I was beginning to regret not going with Dinu and wondered if I could catch him up when the boy's brother called out to him.

'Come on, Plato! We'd best be getting back.'

I stared at him. 'What did he just call you?'

The boy's finger was up the other nostril. 'It's his nickname for me: Plato.'

My jaw dropped.

I quickly did the maths. Socrates died in the year 399 BC aged seventy, when Plato was around twenty-five. This was sixteen years earlier, which would make Socrates' most famous disciple about nine or ten.

It all added up, and my jaw dropped some more.

Most historians rank the philosopher Plato on a par with Shakespeare, Einstein and Beethoven: one of the top-ten great minds ever to have lived.

Could it be that the boy who stood before me picking his nose would grow up to be one of the world's greatest geniuses?

If so, how could I possibly turn down the chance to spend a little time with him?

# 25

# Flat Forehead

The boy's big brother had actually called him 'Plah Tone' but I was pretty sure from Greek class that meant Plato.

'Your name is Plato?' I repeated, just to be sure. We were walking back towards Athens several paces behind his brother, a dark-haired man of about thirty in a cloak made of the same sky-blue cloth as Plato's chiton.

As we passed beneath the arched gate, the boy sighed. 'The name "Plato" is rather brutish, isn't it? The other boys at the palaestra call me that on account of my forehead.'

I nodded, remembering that the word *platys* literally means 'flat' or 'broad'. Like in *platypus*, which means 'flat foot'.

'I'm going to insist my brother stops calling me that.'

'No! Don't!' I cried. 'Plato is a good name. It's so much easier to remember than . . . what did you say your real name was?'

'Aristocles.' He sidestepped to avoid a steaming pile of mule droppings in the road. 'Do you really prefer my nickname?'

'Yes!' I said, conscious that renaming the greatest philosopher in the world might alter the future. 'Claim it with pride.'

Kid Plato nodded solemnly then gave me a sideways glance. 'Tell me about the country you come from?'

For a mad moment I considered telling him about men flying in giant metal birds called aeroplanes and trains that travel underground and buildings taller than the Acropolis. I could also tell him how everybody walks around looking at little metal tablets that fit in the palm of your hand and which allow you to communicate with people all over the world in a nanosecond.

Instead of describing twenty-first-century London, or even third-century Londinium, which wouldn't exist for another eight hundred years, I decided to tell him about a typical Iron Age village like the one we had visited in Year Four.

'Um. We have round houses made of mud-covered woven branches and topped with straw roofs. Nothing like that.' I gestured at a massive stone wall running parallel to the road some distance from it.

'That's one of the Long Walls,' said Kid Plato. 'See the other one way over there?' He pointed. 'They were built as an addition to the city walls to protect the road to and from the port so we can always supply the city. Without them our enemies could besiege us and we would soon starve. Don't you have town walls in your land?'

'Not really.' I tried to remember what they did at Butser Ancient Farm. 'My village has a wooden stake fence which is mainly to keep our animals in and wild animals out.'

'What about your enemies?'

'I live on an island. So that helps.'

'Ah.' He nodded wisely.

Before he could ask me any more about my home I said quickly, 'Tell me more about Athens. You say the war with the Spartans is over?'

'Yes. For the last six years. My brother actually fought in one of the battles. And so did Socrates.'

'Your brother fought beside Socrates?' I said. 'May I ask him about it?'

'*Day-lone hotee,*' he said. Of course.

'Excuse me, sir!' I called out to his brother, who was still several paces in front of us. 'Did you really fight beside Socrates?'

Kid Plato's older brother turned and waited for us to catch up. He had a sturdy body, a broad forehead and keen black eyes, like his brother's. I noticed he held a walking stick in his right hand, as many men did.

'Glaucon, this is . . .' Kid Plato looked at me.

'Alexis,' I said. 'From the Tin Islands. I'm hoping to meet Socrates. Your brother says you fought with him.'

'Yes.' Glaucon fell into step with us. 'Socrates was with us at the Battle of Delium nearly ten years ago. We Athenians had to retreat, but he set the example. He never panicked but kept turning and glaring back fiercely at the enemy behind us.'

He spent the next hour telling me stories of Socrates' bravery and endurance.

He told me how Socrates could walk on ice or frozen ground barefoot. Socrates could stay awake all night without becoming tired and no matter how much wine he drank he never even got tipsy. Once Socrates even risked death to save Alcibiades, who had foolishly charged the enemy in hopes of glory.

'He risked his life to save Alcibiades?' I echoed.

'Yes. He and the general are very close. Socrates used to teach Alcibiades and still longs for him to seek the Good. People call him the wisest man in all Athens but sometimes he could be wiser about his choice of friends. And enemies,' he added.

'Socrates doesn't care about fame or fortune, like Alcibiades,' said Kid Plato. 'He only cares about the soul.'

'Yes,' said Glaucon with a grim expression, 'and one day that could get him killed.'

To my surprise we had already reached the arched gate to the city with its trinket stalls and pleading beggars.

Glaucon reached into his mouth and gave each of the beggars a small coin. Once through the gate I could hear the clinking from the Street of the Marble Workers and I caught the sickly-sweet smell of the Great Drain. I recognised the State Prison and offered up a silent prayer of thanks: if not for Alcibiades we would be there now, awaiting trial.

We turned left and almost bumped into some girls emerging from between the columns of a red-roofed building. They had full water pots on their heads and looked just like some of the girls on Greek vases my gran had taken me to see at the British Museum.

They giggled when they saw us and hurried past.

A few moments later two men overtook us at a run and then skidded to a stop.

'Glaucon!' called the one with curly hair. 'Socrates has gone to hear Hippias give a lecture in the Painted Stoa.'

'You know what Socrates thinks of sophists,' said the one with straight hair. 'This should be fine entertainment. Come on!'

Glaucon turned to his younger brother. 'The shoemaker's shop is just up ahead on the right. You've been once before with me, I think? Wait for me there.' He glanced up at the sky. 'I'll see you in about an hour, at noon.'

He hurried after his friends towards the marketplace.

'Wait!' I said to Kid Plato. 'Did he just say Socrates is in the Agora?'

'*Hoo toce!*' That is so.

'Then let's go!'

'We can't. Children aren't allowed in the Agora.'

'But I was there earlier.'

'Not when the market is on.'

'I don't believe it! That's why I've come all this way.' I recited my talismantra again: 'To seek Socrates, the lover of wisdom, the wisest man in Athens!'

Kid Plato's dark eyes gleamed with excitement. 'Can you run away fast, if necessary?'

'Yes!' I cried. 'I'm excellent at running away.'

# 26
# Smelly Agora

Kid Plato grinned when I said I could run away fast. 'Look – Simon the Shoemaker's house.' He pointed at a two-storey building on our right. I saw a wooden shoe hanging over the open double doors and a shady courtyard within. 'If we get separated, then meet me back here.'

Literally six steps past the door of the shoemaker's shop we came to a line of black-and-white pebbles running across the road, and on our right, a smiling herm. Kid Plato touched the herm's marble chin beneath the painted beard.

As I turned to do the same I saw a boundary stone.

'I AM THE BOUNDARY OF THE AGORA!' it declared in red painted letters on sparkling white marble. It might as well have shouted: 'NO CHILDREN ALLOWED!'

But Kid Plato boldly stepped over the line of pebbles, right foot first. And so did I.

Maybe it was because the blazing sun magnified all the

odours, but the moment we entered the Agora I encountered a symphony of smells.

The sickly-sweet whiff of sewage from the drain behind us formed a base note.

Next came the rhythmic pong of sausage-sellers roasting their ancient hot dogs on portable clay barbeques.

Then the churchy melody of incense drifting from shrines under their sacred trees.

Rising above it all was a chorus of smells coming from the men around us: rank sweat, stale urine, bad breath and perfumed beard oil.

'They said Hippias in the Painted Stoa,' Kid Plato called over his shoulder. 'It's this way.'

'Who's Hippias?'

'Only the richest and most famous sophist in Greece.'

'What's a sophist again?'

Kid Plato waited for me to catch up. 'We Athenians love to discuss things. But even more, we love to argue. And most of all, we love to take people to court to prove we're right and they're wrong.'

'Wrong about what?'

'Boundary stones, ownership of a slave, the nature of the universe . . . it doesn't matter. The point is, we Athenians love to argue in public. Look!'

Without stopping, he pointed at a building beyond the parasol-roofed Tholos. 'That's the Bouleterium. The council house. The seat of our famous democracy and site of even more debates.'

This kid was amazing.

'How old are you?' I asked him.

'Nine. But I was telling you what a sophist is.'

'Go on.'

'A sophist is a man who claims to be able to teach you to speak so persuasively that you will win any argument, whether it's right or wrong. Socrates hates them.'

'Why?'

'Because they're only concerned with money, prestige and power. They don't give two figs about the truth. It's all about their own skill. The sophist Protagoras claims he can win an argument with a worse argument, just by using his skills of persuasion.'

'That sounds like most politicians I know,' I said.

'Yes! Socrates says his divine voice warned him not to go into politics. He says if you want to improve the world, you should do it as an individual.'

But now I wasn't really listening. I was too busy looking.

We were in the heart of the Athenian Agora and it was bonkers.

There were no other kids and only a few women. Everywhere were men, men, men.

Tooth-pullers and fortune tellers squatted on rush mats. Money-changers and scribes sat at folding tables. Fruit and veg sellers stood in the shade cast by reed awnings over their portable stalls.

Wealthy men, those with slaves, wore the tablecloth thing called a himation and most carried a walking stick.

Farmers, salesmen and craftsmen wore the *exomis*, the tunic fastened over the left shoulder that left the right arm free and most of the chest exposed.

The rest of them – beggars, snack sellers, snake charmers, tumblers, jugglers, basket-weavers, storytellers, talisman-makers, curse-breakers and so on – were either totally naked or wearing only a loincloth.

In contrast to the brightly painted temples, people's clothes were pretty dull: mainly brown, beige or cream with the occasional garment of dusty blue or rusty red. And lots of skin: tanned, bronzed, sunburned, olive and nut-brown.

That's why the bright turquoise dress caught my eye.

A girl up ahead was wearing a drab brown headscarf but her dress was unmistakable. There was no other colour like it in the whole of the Agora.

Of course Dinu's annoying little sister hadn't waited patiently in the Parthenon.

She had come to look for us.

A twenty-first-century girl who spoke only a few phrases of Greek, in the male-dominated Agora of Athens?

Pure madness.

## 27

# The Girl in Turquoise

'Crina!' I shouted. 'CRINA!'

The noise of the Agora must have drowned me out because she kept going.

'CRINA!'

Totally forgetting about Kid Plato, I charged after her.

I ran past the fragrant stalls of the garland-makers and pungent tables of garlic and onion.

I wove between pancake sellers standing over sizzling tripods.

I pelted past tables of radishes and peas and bunches of green herbs. I leaped over bowls of olives and cones of ground spices and baskets of little red cherries.

'CRINA!'

For a few moments my nose was flooded with the heady scent of wine as I raced between bulging wineskins and black-glazed amphoras.

Then my ears were filled with twittering as I jogged down a corridor of birds in wicker cages. Birdsong gave way to the buzzing of flies and the smell of blood as I ran through the meat market. Now I was hurrying through the sound of men reading out loud to themselves at the scroll sellers' stalls.

I dodged a beggar with no legs and a dog biting his ticks.

I gave a wide berth to several groups of arguing men and to a snake charmer with an actual cobra.

I leaped over smouldering piles of dog poo, mule dung and cow pats.

I finally stopped, gasping, beside the bronze statue of a naked hero wearing a real himation. But nowhere could I see that distinctive twenty-first-century colour of turquoise.

Just to my left, a man in a loincloth was pulling the tooth of a man kneeling on a mat. A small crowd cheered as he finally succeeded and held the bloody molar aloft. At the same moment I spotted a flash of turquoise out of the corner of my eye.

Crina was going up some broad, flat steps towards a painted temple on a low, tree-studded hill.

I knew that temple. It was the Temple of Hephaestus, the blacksmith god.

I sprinted past an ancient black poplar tree and hurried up the broad steps after her and into a world of ringing metal. There were trees and shrubs up here, planted around the temple. Their glittering leaves seemed to reflect back the bright sound of metalworkers. In the shade of these trees, half-naked men in leather aprons were working bronze and iron: tapping and banging and making the hot metal sizzle in buckets of water.

Then I spotted her. She was standing before one of the blacksmiths. Her head was covered with a brown shawl even though the noonday sun was blazing down.

'Crina!' I came up behind her and grasped her shoulder with my sweaty hand. 'Why didn't you answer me?'

She squealed and whirled to face me.

Then I saw why she had not answered me.

It was not Crina.

It was a girl with frizzy black hair. Eighteen, maybe nineteen years old.

The blacksmith behind her rose to his feet and brandished red-hot tongs.

'What are you doing to my wife?' he growled.

'Nothing!' I stammered, letting go. 'It's just that my friend has a dress exactly like that.'

Then a terrible thought struck me.

What if Crina had not stayed hidden in the depths of the Parthenon?

What if she had ventured out?

And what if the blacksmith's wife had robbed Crina of her dress?

# 28
# Fair Trade

The girl in Crina's dress must have seen the expression on my face because she said, 'Don't worry. Your friend is safe. I found her crying on the stairs leading down from the Acropolis. She kept saying, *You speak the truth, O Socrates*, over and over. So I asked her if she wanted me to take her to the house of Socrates. When she heard his name she said yes. So I did.'

'You took her to Socrates' house?' I said.

'Yes. She wanted to thank me, but she had no coins. So I said I would trade dresses with her.' She fingered the turquoise dress. 'I've never seen cloth this colour. And the weave is so fine.'

'Can you take me to his house too?' I said. 'Or tell me where it is?'

'No need,' panted a young voice behind me. It was Kid Plato, out of breath from running after me. I'd totally forgotten about him. 'Socrates is only a stone's throw from here.'

'Thank the gods!' I was turning to follow him when the blacksmith caught my wrist in a grip like bronze.

'What is this?' he growled. 'It was attached to the peplos your friend gave my wife.' He held out a twenty-first-century label, machine-stitched in English. It read 'Paris Mode Fashions'.

'This is not Greek,' said the blacksmith. A big drop of sweat hung from the tip of his nose. 'I can read enough to know that. Are you a spy? Is this a secret code?'

His wife looked at me with wide eyes. 'Or a curse?'

My first thought was to reassure them that it was harmless. Then I had a better idea.

'I am not a spy,' I said to the blacksmith. Then I turned to his wife. 'But you're right. It's a powerful curse. A curse against theft. If you are telling the truth it won't hurt you, but if you *did* rob my friend, then the spirits will be angry. Are you telling the truth?'

Her eyes grew wider. She glanced at her husband, who stood clutching the label and glowering. Then she looked at the ground.

'It was not her idea to trade, it was mine,' she whispered. Then she looked up. 'But I did take her to Socrates' house, I swear. His wife Xanthippe opened the door. And I left your friend there, I promise.'

'You're sure she's safe at Socrates' house?'

She touched an amulet around her neck. 'I swear by Artemis Brauronia I'm telling the truth.'

'Give me the label. I will say a magic phrase and then burn it so that you will be free of any guilt or blame.'

Reluctantly the blacksmith handed his wife the cloth label and she quickly thrust it into my hand.

I stepped closer to the blacksmith's fire and dropped the label onto the coals. To make it seem more mysterious and convincing, I recited the *Our Father* prayer in rapid English while waving my hands over the burning scrap.

The blacksmith and his wife stared at me. So did Kid Plato.

Once I was sure all evidence of the twenty-first century had been reduced to ashes, I nodded my head. 'Now you are safe. No evil can harm you.'

I turned away and then turned back. 'How do you know Socrates, anyway?' I asked.

The girl and her husband exchanged a look and for the first she smiled. 'Everybody in Athens knows who Socrates is.'

Kid Plato tugged my tunic. 'Come on,' he said. 'Everybody may know *who* he is, but I just told you: I know *where* he is right now.'

## 29
# Seeking Socrates

As Kid Plato and I hurried down from the Temple of Hephaestus, I noticed what I hadn't noticed on my way up: the wide flat steps doubled as seats. About twenty men were now sitting there, listening to a man giving a speech.

I thought I heard the orator mention Alcibiades so I slowed down to listen, but Kid Plato hooked his elbow in mine the way I had seen other men do. 'Come on! Or we might miss him.'

We trotted past the ranked columns of two stoas, then vaulted the Great Drain and cut through a small grove of olive and bay trees. The trees had bits of wool tied to their branches. As we passed a square enclosure, I glimpsed an altar through a permanently open gap in the wall. Some skinny men were sitting in a small patch of shade at its base.

Kid Plato saw me looking and said, 'That's the Altar of

Pity, where runaway slaves and other criminals can take refuge.'

I made a mental note to remember the Altar of Pity the next time I was being chased.

Emerging from the dusty shade of the little grove, we came back into blazing sunshine. Six paths met here and each had a herm. A few were wooden, but most were marble and all of them had the painted, bearded face of Hermes atop a short square column.

Kid Plato wiped his sweaty forehead with the back of his arm. 'This crossroads is called the Herms, for obvious reasons. And that's the Painted Stoa.' He pointed straight ahead to a stoa with brightly painted lions-head rainspouts above the white columns. Men were spilling out of it and down the steps.

Kid Plato's small shoulders slumped. 'It looks as if we're too late.'

'Why?'

'Here comes Hippias. And he's blushing! The ultimate disgrace.'

'Is it?'

Kid Plato nodded. 'Here in Athens a man would rather die than lose face. I suspect Socrates is behind this.'

Hippias the sophist was a thin man with a nose like a hatchet and a wreath on his balding head. He was mopping his forehead with a corner of a dusty pink himation the same colour as his flushed cheeks. A group of grim-faced young men hurried after him.

'Those are his students,' whispered Kid Plato. 'They're the richest of the rich.'

In contrast with Hippias's unsmiling entourage, the other men coming down out of the stoa were laughing and chatting happily. Some moved away into the Agora while others lingered by the columns.

'Look,' I said. 'There's your brother.'

Glaucon and his two friends stood on the top step in animated conversation.

We went up the steps, and Kid Plato tugged his brother's himation. 'What happened?'

As Glaucon turned, his smile became a scowl. 'You shouldn't be here!' he hissed. 'I told you to wait at Simon's.'

But one of his friends – the one with straight hair – grabbed Kid Plato's shoulders. 'You should have heard it, Plato. Socrates was brilliant! He got Hippias to admit that Achilles is more cunning than Odysseus–'

'–which was the exact opposite of Hippias's original thesis,' interrupted the other friend, the one with curly hair.

'And then,' said Straight Hair, 'Socrates banged his staff on the floor and proclaimed: *According to what you have just said, dear Hippias, a deceptive liar is the best sort of man.*'

'*Oh Socrates! How can that possibly be true?*' harrumphed Curly, obviously imitating Hippias.

'*I don't know,*' said Straight Hair as a beaming Socrates, '*but we seem to have just proved it!*'

Curly pretended to splutter and stammer.

Straight Hair imitated Socrates by leaning on an imaginary staff. '*It's no surprise that I, being ignorant and slow, have got in a muddle. But if a wise sophist like yourself gets confused then we have a grave problem, do we not?*'

They all burst out laughing, even Glaucon. He ruffled his brother's hair. 'He's still in there if you want to introduce your friend. But meet me at Simon's in half an hour!'

'Thank you, Glaucon!' Kid Plato pulled me into the stoa before I could thank him too.

Coming out of the blazing sun into the shade of the stoa was a huge relief. It was almost cool and there was even a slight breeze. The space was still crowded with at least two hundred men, mostly wearing the light tablecloth himation. They were standing in groups, laughing and talking.

Kid Plato hooked his elbow in mine again and pulled me through the crowd. A few men glared at us or tutted, but most just moved aside. As we pushed past men, the combined stench of their sweaty armpits nearly overpowered me. I had to breathe through my mouth.

A stocky man dripping with sweat said loudly, 'Socrates is nothing more than a sophist himself.'

Kid Plato stopped and turned. 'You are wrong, sir. Socrates is different from the sophists in three respects. First, he never charges money. Second, he cares about the truth. And third, he uses words as tools to seek the truth. Unless he's showing how hollow the so-called skills of the sophists really are.'

The man stared at Kid Plato, open-mouthed. 'Should you even be here?' he spluttered at last.

It was my turn to hook my elbow in Kid Plato's and pull him on, but before we reached Socrates we heard another couple of men.

'. . . serves that pompous sophist right. He charges a fortune to teach boys wool fluff.'

'But Socrates has made a powerful enemy,' said the other.

I could see Kid Plato pressing his lips together, but the last statement had made me think.

I leaned over and whispered, 'If Socrates is so wise, why does he humiliate powerful men. Isn't that dangerous?'

'Yes. But he doesn't care. He's on a mission to expose pretentious liars. He wants people to think for themselves. He often compares himself to a horsefly stinging the sluggish city into wakefulness. And he cares more about virtue and truth than his own safety. You'll see.'

When we reached the back of the stoa my eyes widened. The whole back wall was painted with a scene of Greeks dropping out of the Trojan horse and setting Troy on fire.

Kid Plato tugged my tunic again. 'Look! There's Socrates. Talking to those men.'

Some men moved aside and I recognised him immediately.

You know Santa Claus from the Coke ads? With his round cheeks and snub nose and jolly smile? Take off his hat and boots and all his clothes, send him to Muscle Beach for a year to lift weights under a blazing sun and then put him in a threadbare grey himation that shows off his hard-as-rock arms and his leathery brown skin.

That was what my first glimpse of Socrates made me think of: tanned Santa wearing nothing but a threadbare tablecloth and leaning on a staff.

## 30
# Santa in a Tablecloth

I had done it. I had found the man I'd been sent to find.

All I had to do was get a few soundbites from him. Then I could go back home, collect my money, become an avatar on the coolest computer game in history and sit back to enjoy a life of fame and fortune.

We moved closer in order to hear what the wisest man in the world was saying. He was speaking with a young man in a dusty pink himation, the same colour as the one Hippias had been wearing.

'One of Hippias's disciples, no doubt,' whispered Kid Plato in my ear.

'Tell me, Lysias, son of Hippomachus,' Socrates was saying, 'do not all men want to be happy?'

'Of course!' said the young man. With his bronze-coloured hair and skin he reminded me of a famous statue called *The Charioteer*.

'Then how can we be happy?'

'I don't understand the question.'

'Will we be happy if we have good things?'

'Of course.'

'And what sorts of things make us happy? Wealth, health and physical beauty?'

'All those things.'

Socrates smiled encouragingly. 'How about good birth, power and honour?'

'Those too.'

'What about self-control, justice and courage?'

'Also good.'

'And what about wisdom? Is it not the greatest of those good things?'

The young man frowned. 'What do you mean?'

'Say we had lots of food but did not eat it, would that good thing benefit us?'

'*Ooda moce*,' he said. No way.

'Or take a craftsman – a shoemaker, for example. If he had leather and cork and adzes and awls but left them to one side, would they be of any use to him?'

'No use at all.'

'And if a person had all the good things we mentioned above – wealth, power, courage – but did not make use of them, would he be happy simply because he possessed them?'

'*Ooda moce*,' he said again. No way.

'So shall we say that those good things will only benefit a person if they use them?'

'That seems right.'

'But is that enough?'

'What do you mean, Socrates?'

'What if he uses them wrongly? The shoemaker, say. If he were to try to make a tunic from leather and cork using awls and adzes. Or if the brave man mustered up his courage and raced to certain death.'

'Why, then those good things would be worse than useless.'

'So do you agree that the wrong use of a thing is worse than the non-use?'

'I do.'

'And the best use of a thing is when it is used rightly?'

'Of course.'

'And in the use of those other things we mentioned — wealth, health, courage and so on — isn't it wisdom that directs us in the best use of them?'

'Yes.'

'So, in themselves they are worth nothing or even less than nothing. But only when used with wisdom can they bring happiness.'

'Yes.'

'Can we then conclude that, to be happy, a man must seek wisdom before all other things?'

'Yes!' The young man's tanned face shone, making him

look even more like bronze.

'Now,' said Socrates, looking around happily, 'shall we discuss how to get wisdom?'

I think he might have gone on for hours but at that moment he caught sight of me and his bug eyes widened. They were twinkly and bright and I could almost feel invisible beams coming from his eyes to mine, like a fishing line drawing me closer. Then his gaze slid beyond me to Kid Plato and his smile grew wider.

'Ah! Young Plato!' he said, and beckoned us both forward.

People were taking this opportunity to leave, and as a man crept away, I noticed the only other kid I had seen so far in the whole Agora. He sat on a marble bench behind Socrates with his head in his hands. From his grubby tunic and shaggy brown hair I guessed he was a slave. But something about him was oddly familiar.

'It is good to see you again,' Socrates said to Kid Plato as we approached. 'And who is your friend?'

'My name is Alexis, son of Philippos.'

Up close I could see that Socrates wasn't as old as Santa. He looked to be about forty-five years old. I was wondering if ancient Greeks shook hands upon meeting.

But I never found out.

The boy on the bench had lifted his head to look at me.

It wasn't a slave boy.

It was Crina with her hair cut short.

# 31
# The Gritty City

Crina saw me at the same moment I spotted her.

'Oh, Alex!' She jumped up and threw her arms around me and squeezed so hard I could barely breathe. 'Thank God you're all right!'

At last she pulled back. 'I saw those strange archers grab you and Dinu and I thought they might have taken you to jail or even the silver mines! Can you ever forgive me for hiding when the guards came? Wait! Where's Dinu?' She looked over my shoulder.

'He's fine. And of course I forgive you. Hiding was the best thing you could have done. But why didn't you stay in the temple, where you were safe?' I tried not to stare. She looked so different with short hair.

'I had to find you and try to save you.'

'Didn't you get the message from a slave? To wait in the temple?'

She shook her head, her eyes brimming.

'Crina, did something happen? Did someone hurt you?'

'No,' she sniffed, 'but it's horrible here! People poo and pee in the streets. And they kill animals and just leave them bleeding on the altars. And there are flies everywhere. And Alex! I saw a *dead body* just lying in the road!'

'But apart from it being ancient Athens, you're OK?'

She nodded and looked up at me with liquid brown eyes and then she finally gave in to tears.

I pulled her back into a hug and patted her back as she sobbed.

This was a side of Crina I had never seen. Comforting her made me feel protective and strong.

And that was a side of me I had never seen.

Kid Plato was talking to Socrates in a low voice and they were both glancing at us.

'She's never been this far from home,' I said to Socrates in my best Greek. 'And she doesn't understand the language.'

Crina stopped crying and stood back and wiped her nose with her forearm, a very un-Crina like thing to do. Strangely, the short hair made her seem prettier than her girlish plaits had done.

Socrates raised his eyebrows at me. 'Your friend sought refuge with me this morning and begged to be allowed to come to the Agora with me.'

Crina said, 'Will you tell Socrates I want to thank him

for looking after me? And also his wife? They were both very kind. She agreed to cut my hair to make me look like a boy. And she gave me this old chiton.'

'My friend Crina says thank you for your hospitality,' I said to Socrates. 'And the chiton.'

'She is most welcome! But our Athenian hospitality is not exhausted.' He put his hand on Kid Plato's shoulder. 'Young Plato tells me you hope to meet your friend at Simon's house. I am a frequent guest but I have not been to see him for several days. I'm due for a visit.'

'Did he just say Plato?' asked Crina. 'As in "Play-Doh"?'

'Yup. That kid picking his nose will grow up to be one of the greatest minds in the history of humanity. By the way,' I added, 'they're going to take us to meet Dinu.'

'Oh, thank God. Once we're all together, can we go back home?'

The relief of finding her was enormous and I suddenly felt happy. 'I thought you wanted to see what ancient Athens looked like?' I teased.

'And now I want to go home!'

'The portal won't open until midnight, another twelve hours from now.'

'Oh no! I don't think I can bear it.' Her tummy growled fiercely.

'Crina,' I said, 'have you had anything to eat?'

'Of course not. We're not allowed.'

'We're not allowed to go through the portal with clothes either. Especially not clothes that have a label on them from the twenty-first century,' I said. 'But you did that.'

'Oh no!' She covered her mouth with her free hand. 'Did I leave the label on?'

I turned to Socrates, who was still watching us intently. 'I think some food will cheer her up,' I said.

He rolled his bug eyes in a way that almost made me laugh. 'My wife tried to give her something,' he said, 'but the girl refused to eat!'

'She'll eat now, I think. Do you know where we can get food?'

'Certainly!' Socrates thumped his staff on the marble floor of the stoa. 'I know the best sausage-seller in the Agora. His stall is on the way to Simon's.'

'I'm afraid my friend is a vegetarian,' I said.

'By the dog!' he exclaimed. 'Are you Pythagoreans?'

I wasn't sure what a Pythagorean was so I tipped my head to one side. 'A little bit?'

'Then we'll look out for a bread-seller on the way. Follow me!' And with a swirl of his grubby grey himation, the great philosopher Socrates stepped out of the shady stoa and into the noontime blaze of the marketplace.

'Where's Dinu, again?' asked Crina as we followed him back out into the furnace of the Agora.

'Hopefully at the house of Simon the Shoemaker,' I

whispered. 'Where we're headed now. We'll find you some food, spend a bit of time with Socrates and then get the midnight portal home. Simples.'

But when you go back to the past, nothing is simples.

# 32
# Pelican Walk

When Dinu and I were doing the intensive Greek course in the villa outside Rome, one of our instructors had told us that Socrates was famous for walking like a pelican.

I have never seen a pelican walk, but there are plenty of geese in Wandsworth, especially down by the river, and that's exactly what he looked like. He strutted along, his walking stick in his right hand and his left arm held away from his body and pointing backwards, the way some men walk but no woman ever seems to. The soles of his bare feet were almost black and I could see the tanned bald patch on top of his head. His head swung right and left as he greeted people or heard them call out to him.

Shoppers and stall-keepers called out greetings with cheerful smiles, although a few men glared and shook their heads. One thing was clear: everybody knew him.

Here in the marketplace of Athens he was as much a celebrity as Alcibiades.

A garlic-seller parted his display-curtain of onions and stuck his head through. 'Hey, Socrates!' he cried. 'They say you punctured Hippias's pomposity just now like a spear pops a bladder ball!'

'Sent him back to Elis, I hope!' added the bean-seller in the stall next door.

'Socrates is just as bad as those sophists!' growled a melon farmer from the other side of the path.

'No, he's not!' cried the garlic seller. 'Hippias charges a fortune to teach the skills of rhetoric, but Socrates never accepts as much as an obol.'

Suddenly Socrates said, 'I see the bread-seller!' He lifted his staff and waved it. 'Over here!' he cried, and a moment later we saw a man with a big platter coming towards us.

Socrates reached into his mouth. I was no longer astonished to see that it held a coin. But Crina was.

'He keeps coins in his mouth?' she gasped.

'Yup. Sometimes in their belt, but mostly in their mouths. Especially small change.'

'But that's so unhygienic!'

'They don't know about germs, remember?'

'But still . . . in your *mouth*? What if you swallowed it?'

'I guess there's nowhere else to put it.' I gestured around us. 'Look at them all! It's so hot here that most men are wearing the equivalent of a thin T-shirt or light tablecloth.'

'If that!' She averted her eyes from a naked juggler.

But before the bread-seller could reach us, a sweaty man with a bushy black beard and a brick-red himation loomed up.

'Children are not allowed in the Agora!' the man shouted at Socrates.

'I know, I know!' said Socrates, holding up his free hand, palm outwards. 'I'm taking them out.'

The man opened his mouth to say something more but the sound of galloping hoofs made us all turn.

'By Zeus!' cried the man. 'A *chariot*! That's even worse than children.'

Sure enough, a chariot had entered the Agora and was thundering straight for us.

That blood-chilling image is forever frozen in my memory. Two horses – one white and one black – galloping straight at us.

And the most terrifying thing of all?

Dinu was driving.

# 33
# Garlands of Praise

The chariot showed no sign of stopping.

The angry man in the brick-red himation dived into a nearby basket display but Socrates barked a command: 'Don't move!'

The bearded philosopher stood still as a statue, gripping his walking stick in one hand and Kid Plato's shoulder in the other. Crina and I cowered behind him.

At the last possible moment, the two horses were pulled up so hard that they actually skidded on their rears. A great cloud of dust rose up around us and the entire Agora went quiet, waiting to see the carnage that would be revealed when it settled.

When the air around us cleared we saw the two snorting horses standing an arm's length away from Socrates, who had not budged.

Dinu's face was as white as Parian marble.

But behind him Alcibiades was laughing. 'I knew you could do it!' He jumped down then helped Dinu down too.

'Dinu!' Crina ran to her brother and threw her arms around him. Just as well – he might have collapsed without her support. I arrived just in time to give him a hand.

'Are you OK?' I asked.

He gave me a grin. 'Wobbly knees,' he said, and then, 'Wasn't that the best thing ever?'

'Best thing ever?' I echoed in disbelief.

Crina gave him a thump on the arm. 'You nearly killed us!'

'He's so cool!' said Dinu. 'He let me drive the chariot and later he's going to take me to the palaestra and teach me to use a sword!'

'Who *is* he?' Crina had turned to look at Alcibiades, who had thrown his arms around Socrates. 'He looks like a Greek god.'

But I didn't need to tell her. Around us men in the marketplace were beginning to chant his name.

A laughing Socrates pulled away from Alcibiades' embrace and said, 'Come with us to Simon's! My young friend Plato is meeting his brother there.'

'That's just where we were headed,' said Alcibiades. He nodded a greeting first at me and then at Kid Plato, who he obviously recognised. Then he spotted Crina and his eyebrows went up.

'I assume this is your sister Crina, dressed as a boy?'

Crina was gazing back at him, speechless.

'She doesn't speak much Greek,' I explained. 'And she doesn't know the ways of this city very well.'

Alcibiades cocked his head. 'Well, why don't you children ride? Socrates and I will lead the team.'

He took the bridle of the black horse and Socrates went to help guide the white. Kid Plato, Dinu, Crina and I dutifully crammed ourselves into the bouncy chariot.

The men around us were still chanting the name of Alcibiades, and as we rolled forward, some began tossing flower garlands at us. We each caught one and put it on. Cool leaves of ivy tickled my forehead and the heady scent of rose made me dizzy.

Up ahead, Alcibiades, now wearing three garlands, turned his head and I heard him call out to Socrates, 'The sweetest of all sounds is praise.'

I didn't hear Socrates' reply, but as we rode out of the Agora to the cheers of the people, I remember thinking: *He's not wrong.*

We could still hear the chanting of adoring crowds as we jumped off the back of the chariot and went through open double doors into the house of Simon the Shoemaker.

'I'll be with you in a moment,' called Alcibiades. 'I just need to find someone to take my team home.'

The courtyard was blissfully cool after the baking hot street, and it smelled pleasantly of leather, beeswax and pine resin. The noonday sun shone through a thickly woven grapevine trellis overhead and filled the space with soft green light. For a moment I felt like a fish in an aquarium.

No wonder people liked hanging out here.

At the right-hand end of the courtyard was something like a fat ceramic upside-down top hat.

In the middle of this space was a wooden bench with rush mats rolled up underneath. Two people were sitting on the bench. Glaucon, the older brother of Kid Plato. And a stocky man in an *exomis* that showed his shoulders, back and chest felted with black hair.

Away to the left were five children. They sat on rush mats in 'cobblers' pose', which I know from Gran making me do yoga. One was cutting leather, two were tapping in hobnails, and two were stitching. I was surprised to see that two of them were girls.

Then reality doused me like a bucket of ice water.

They were child slaves.

# 34

# A Load of Young Cobblers

'Welcome, Socrates! And welcome to your young disciples!' The stocky guy rose from the bench in the centre of the courtyard and came towards us. Like Socrates he was balding, but his hair and beard were black, not grey. In a city of dark, bearded men, his most noticeable feature was his single black eyebrow. 'I see you are all wearing garlands. Have you just come from some festival?'

'No, dear Simon,' replied Socrates. 'We've just been bathing in the reflected glory of Alcibiades.'

One of the slave cobblers, a black-haired girl about my age, got up and came over to Socrates. Then she bent at the waist to squint down at his feet.

'Alas, Simona!' Socrates hung his head. 'I'm not wearing my beautiful sandals! I'm afraid I'm barefoot as usual.'

She stood upright again and gave him a cross-eyed look from beneath straight black eyebrows that met over her nose. At first I thought she was trying to be funny. Then I realised she really did have a squint.

'Here.' Socrates removed his garland and gently placed it on her head. 'You deserve it more than I.'

Simona snatched the garland from her head and sent it spinning towards an altar in the corner of the courtyard behind the cobblers. Then she turned back to Socrates, still wearing her scowl.

'Do you ever wear the shoes I made for you?' she demanded in a very un-slave-like manner.

'He wore them to Agathon's party last year,' said thrice-garlanded Alcibiades as he came striding into the courtyard. 'But I've not seen them on his feet since then.'

'General Alcibiades! What an honour! Come in! Come in!' Simon the Shoemaker bowed to Alcibiades and then turned to the cross-eyed girl.

'Simona!' he said. 'Bring some wine and bread for our guests.'

Simona gave Alcibiades an even fiercer glare than she'd given Socrates and stomped off towards the nearest doorway.

'You must forgive her,' Simon the Shoemaker said. 'She's as hot-tempered as her mother was.'

Alcibiades took off two of his three garlands and handed them to Simon. 'I've just sent my chariot back home with a good-looking youth by the name of Xenophon,' he said. 'Do any of you know if he is trustworthy?'

'Yes, indeed,' said Socrates. 'Xenophon, son of Gryllus, is only fifteen but he is already a gifted horseman. Your team is in safe hands.'

'Helena!' Simon the Shoemaker snapped his fingers at the other young slaves. 'Put these garlands on our altar. Then go help your sister. Castor! Pollux! Bring some food. Paulos! Draw some water from the well and help our guests wash their dusty feet and hands.'

As the other girl and twin boys went to help Simona, the youngest boy put down his hammer and ran to the other end of the courtyard. They all had monobrows just like Simon. I realised this must be a family business and that Simon's workers were his children, rather than his slaves. But was that any better?

Little Paulos was lowering a leather bucket into the fat upside-down top hat made of clay, which must be a well head.

Alcibiades went over to him and let the boy pour some water on his feet. Then the handsome general bent to dip his hands in the bucket and splash water on his face. He stood up, face shining and short beard dripping. Wearing his garland and smelling not unpleasantly of sweat mixed with musky perfume, he reminded me of Dionysus, the god of wine.

The rest of us queued up to follow his example. I was

last. When I bent to splash my face, the garland on my head almost fell into the bucket. I placed it on Paulos's head and he gave a big smile in return. His two front teeth were just coming in, so I guessed he was about seven.

Simona and Helena came back into the cool courtyard holding something like a ceramic punchbowl between them. I remembered from many museum visits with my gran that this type of vase was a krater, for mixing water and wine. The silent twins followed, carrying a low wooden table with bread, hard-boiled eggs and little saucers of salt crystals. They rolled out the rush mats for us kids to sit on, while Socrates and Alcibiades and Glaucon took the bench. Simon hovered nearby, making sure everyone was being looked after.

Simona dipped a big skyphos into the krater and handed it to Socrates with a shy smile. The philosopher poured out a dribble as a libation, then drank and passed it to Alcibiades, who passed it to Glaucon, who handed it across the table to his brother. Kid Plato, sitting cross-legged beside us, passed the cup to Dinu, who passed it to me. It was well-watered and surprisingly refreshing.

Crina stared at me in disbelief as I held the skyphos out to her.

'But it's *wine*,' she hissed. 'And you've all drunk from it!'

'Think of it as Communion at church,' I whispered. When she still hesitated, I said, 'It's diluted. Plus wine kills bacteria. It makes the water safe to drink.'

She took a tiny sip, then smiled and took a bigger sip.

Everyone was now tucking into the food so I handed her a wedge of bread.

'Here. Take this bread and dip it in the wine,' I whispered.

Crina glanced up questioningly at Simona, who gave a cross-eyed smile and inclined her head.

Crina dipped the bread in the wine and took her first bite of food in nearly three days. Her eyes closed and she smiled with pleasure.

'*Kalos.*' Good. She mopped up the last of the wine and passed the empty skyphos up to Simona. 'Thank you,' she said in Greek.

Simona refilled the cup and then put it in the centre of the low table so anyone could drink or dip. I noticed it had the name SIMON scratched in the black glaze of the base.

'So!' Alcibiades turned his blue gaze on me. 'You have come all this way to meet Socrates! Did he tell you the oracle at Delphi proclaimed him the wisest man in the world?'

I was suddenly a little bit star-struck to find his attention focused on me. Before I could recite our talismantra, Alcibiades slapped Socrates on the back.

'Of course he didn't! He's far too modest. But I will. A few years ago a friend of his went to the oracle at Delphi to ask if there was anyone wiser than Socrates. The god Apollo, speaking through the Pythia, said, "No one".'

Socrates brushed wine-soaked crumbs from his beard

and looked around at us with his bright bug eyes. 'No one was more astonished than I to hear Apollo call me wise. But when I questioned the citizens here in Athens in order to disprove the oracle I realised that I *am* wiser than them. But only in one respect. They all think they know something when they don't. Whereas I know that I know nothing.'

Everyone laughed, but Alcibiades held up his hand for silence and then brought it down firmly on Socrates' brown shoulder.

'This man,' he proclaimed, 'is much more than the wisest man in the world. He is a sorcerer!'

# 35
# The Socratic Method

Crina frowned. 'What is a "go-ace"?' she whispered, repeating the sounds of the word Alcibiades had used to describe Socrates.

'It means a sorcerer, male witch or magician,' I said. 'It can also mean a cheat.'

Being described as a magician didn't seem to bother Socrates, who was peeling a hard-boiled egg.

But Kid Plato came to his defence. 'Do you mean to say Socrates is a trickster?'

'I don't know!' Alcibiades threw up his hands dramatically. 'All I know is that whenever I am in the presence of this man something amazing happens to me.'

He looked around at us with an expression of wonder in his kohl-lined eyes. 'He makes me feel ashamed! He alone can make me feel that way. He makes me want to seek the good of my soul. But then I am seduced by the cheers of the crowd. So I flee him, like a runaway slave. Like a coward!'

We all looked at Socrates as he plucked a single long hair from his beard, looped it around the egg and pulled it tight to slice the egg neatly in half.

'This man,' continued Alcibiades, 'is unlike any human being of the past or present. He's like one of those little figures of Silenus you can buy in the potters' quarter – the ones that open up to reveal a treasure inside.'

'We have one of those!' cried Simona. She hurried to the shrine in the corner and came back with a painted wooden figurine. It was as big as my two fists pressed together and showed a squatting figure playing pan pipes. With its bald head, big lips, snub nose and bug eyes, it did bear an almost uncanny resemblance to Socrates. Except for the pointy ears.

'Isn't that a satyr?' I asked.

'Of course!' cried Kid Plato. 'Silenus is the wise old father of satyrs.'

Simona cried, 'Look!' and she cracked open the figurine to reveal a smaller figure inside. It reminded me of a Kinder Egg.

'Apollo!' said Crina. Everyone nodded encouragingly at her.

I added, 'Playing his lyre.'

Alcibiades took the wooden figure from Simona, closed it and held it up next to Socrates. 'See? This Silenus is the perfect metaphor for Socrates. He looks ordinary outside, even ugly. But inside there is something divine.'

'Silenus was also the tutor of Dionysus,' added Kid Plato.

Alcibiades turned to Socrates, who was brushing bits of egg from his beard. 'Go on, then!' he said. 'Show them. Do what you do!'

Socrates nodded slowly, then turned to look down at me and Dinu and Crina and Kid Plato and the mini-cobblers behind us. We all sat on the rush mats, gazing up at him.

'Tell me then, children,' Socrates hooked his hands around one knee and leaned back, 'what do you all desire?'

As I whispered the translation into Crina's ear, little Paulos and Helena cried out in unison: '*Eudaimonia!*'

I guessed they had played this game before.

'*Eudaimonia*,' I explained to Crina, 'is often translated as "happiness", but Gran says it means "contentment". Like doing what you're meant to do in your life.'

Socrates waited politely for me to translate. Then he said, 'The little ones have given a good reply. What else do we desire?'

Dinu raised his hand. 'Fame and riches,' he said. 'That's what I desire in life.' He glanced at Alcibiades, who gave a small nod of approval.

Kid Plato said nothing. He merely watched us with his inscrutable dark eyes.

Socrates tipped his head to one side and looked at Dinu. 'By "fame", do you mean *kleos*, the glory that comes with beating an enemy, or notoriety, a reputation for doing something not glorious at all?'

'Either,' said Dinu happily. 'I just want to be famous!'

'So you don't mind if everyone knows you as the boy who tripped at the starting block of the race and broke both hips?'

Everyone burst out laughing and I had to translate for Crina.

Even in the green light of the courtyard I could see Dinu's cheeks flush beneath his garland. 'Obviously not that.'

'Or say you accidentally burned down the Parthenon? In that case your name would be famous for all of time.'

'*Kleos*, then,' said Dinu. 'I want *kleos* fame.'

Socrates stroked his grey beard. 'Are you aware that to gain *kleos* you must fight well in a battle or speak persuasively at the Assembly? Both those things require much training. Often months. Years, even. Unless your act of glory is some great sacrifice, like Pheidippides who ran all the way from the plain of Marathon and then dropped dead from the effort.'

'Forget about fame then,' said Dinu, taking a gulp of watered wine. 'I'll just have riches.'

'Why do you want to be rich?'

'So I can be happy.'

Socrates frowned. 'How can riches make you happy?'

This question seemed to take Dinu by surprise. He glanced at Alcibiades, who raised his eyebrows. 'Well, being rich would give me lots of time to play games and eat whatever I like and have people wait on me.'

'By "games", do you mean training for the Olympic or Panathenaic Games? Running, jumping, throwing the discus?'

Dinu frowned. 'No. By games I mean battling Spartans . . .'

I knew he wanted to say, 'in a computer game'.

Instead he finished by saying, 'in my imagination'.

'So your idea of happiness, of *eudaimonia*, is to sit around playing imaginary battles while people wait on you, bringing you your favourite food and drink?'

Dinu grinned. '*Day-lon hotee!*' Of course.

'And after a few months of playing imaginary games and gorging yourself, what would you look like?'

'Probably fat and pale, but it doesn't matter. People will like me because I'm rich.'

'But won't your friends only like you for your money?'

Dinu's smile faltered. 'Maybe a few, but not all.'

'Don't you want people to like you for the beauty of your soul, not for your wealth or fame?'

Dinu shrugged. 'How can someone's soul be beautiful? It's inside.' Then he muttered, 'As long as I'm rich and famous, I don't care.'

But he hung his head and his garland fell off.

I could tell Socrates' questions had got to him.

'Don't you see?' said Socrates gently. 'The soul is the only important part of us. That's why I spend every day trying to persuade both young and old to make their soul as good as it can be. The only thing you should think about is whether you are acting rightly or wrongly, to keep your soul pure.'

I raised my hand. 'Do you say that because you believe that our souls are eternal?'

'Some, like the Pythagoreans, say that the soul of man never perishes but can be born again into another body, depending on how we lived. But even if they're mistaken, I believe we should live our lives in the utmost holiness.'

Alcibiades leaned across the low table and grasped Dinu's shoulder. 'Have you ever seen a soul? No. But I'll wager you've seen statues to heroes. Stay with me here in Athens. I'll train you in all the ways of battle. Then you can fight beside me. You'll be my right-hand man. Together we'll gain *kleos*, the good kind of fame, and your name will be known forever.'

Dinu gazed at him with shining eyes.

'What?' said Crina. 'What's happening?'

'Your brother is thinking of staying here instead of going back home.'

'Dinu!' she cried. 'You can't! Apart from everything else, what about the months that will be cut off your life expectancy?'

He shrugged. 'Geoff and Jeff told us that only kicks in when you come back. I could live a long life here.'

I couldn't believe it.

My best mate was seriously tempted to stay in the past so he could live out the real-life version of *Ancient Greek Assassins*.

I opened my mouth to list all the reasons why this would be a terrible decision, but before I could speak someone ran in through the open doors. It was Xanthus, the brown-haired slave, out of breath.

'Master,' he panted, kneeling before Alcibiades. 'I can't find the girl Crina anywhere. But while I was searching for her, I overheard a priest talking. They say you mocked the Mysteries of Kore last night. They have called an emergency assembly and guards are on their way to arrest you now.'

Then he turned and pointed at me and Dinu.

'They're wanted too. The priest says they robbed the temple, tricked some guards into letting them go and then also took part in mocking the Mysteries.'

# 36
# Red Tape

Xanthus the slave boy was obviously terrified.

But it wasn't us he was worried about. It was Alcibiades.

'Master!' Xanthus grabbed his master's hand and tried to pull him up from the bench. 'Come! Now!'

Alcibiades laughed. 'How can I run away? I'm about to lead a fleet of two hundred ships to Syracuse.'

From the street outside a voice boomed, 'All citizens of Athens! Emergency Assembly is called. The Mysteries have been mocked. To the Pnyx. I repeat: the Mysteries have been mocked! To the Pnyx!'

Alcibiades leaped to his feet. 'I shall speak to them now!'

Before any of the rest of us could react, he was off his bench and out the door.

'Master, wait!' Xanthus went to chase after him, with Dinu close behind.

But somehow Socrates had reached the door first and was blocking their exit with his walking stick and a stern voice.

'Is this true?' He looked from Xanthus to Dinu and finally to me. 'Did you mock the ceremony last night?'

'It didn't feel mocking,' I said. 'It was very dignified.'

'But did you hear the gong, drink the *kykeon* and look in the basket?'

'We only pretended to drink the *kykeon*,' I said. 'And we never saw a basket.'

'Did Alcibiades not explain the import of what you were doing?'

'Not exactly.' Dinu and I exchanged an uneasy look.

Socrates shook his head with a sigh, but lowered the stick. Through the doorway beyond him we could see a mass of people hurrying past.

'Friend, we must go,' said Simon the Shoemaker, 'or we will be marked with red.'

'Very well,' said Socrates.

'Glaucon, may we go too?' pleaded Kid Plato.

'No,' said Glaucon, but Socrates held up a hand.

'I think it would be good for your brother to take our young guests to watch. They can see Athenian democracy in action.' Socrates turned back to Kid Plato. 'But wait until the red ropes have passed.'

Simon chose one of several staffs leaning against the wall by the front door, then turned to Simona with a grave expression. 'Once we've left, close the doors and bar them. The shop is closed for the rest of the day.'

'Yes, Father,' she said.

The three men hurried out into the street and we kids crowded into the doorway to watch. The street was full of people – mostly men, all hurrying away from the Agora.

'What are the "red ropes"?' I asked Kid Plato.

'Public slaves follow the crowds,' he explained, 'the way beaters drive animals into a net on the hunt. They carry ropes dipped in wet red dye. If you're a citizen and get dye on your clothes, it marks you out as lazy or reluctant, and you can be fined.'

'What's happening?' Crina asked me.

I told her, and added, 'If they go too slowly, they get red on their clothes.'

'Look!' Little Paulos pointed. 'I see them!'

The crowd was moving faster now and some of the men at the back looked panicked. Then I spotted two stripy archers holding what looked like a dripping red tape between them.

'Oh, I see them,' said Crina.

'Simona!' cried Helena. 'Close the doors like Father told you! Quickly!'

But it seemed her warning came too late. A skinny, frizzy-haired man was turning into the shop, and a surge of others looked ready to follow.

# 37
# Emergency Assembly

'**S**top!' cried Simona, trying to hold back the frizzy-haired young man.

She was strong, but Dinu was stronger.

He shoved Frizzy Hair back onto the street.

The rest of us kids got the doors closed and lowered the crossbeam, a solid plank of oak.

Then we all stood panting with our backs against the door.

Xanthus turned to Simona. 'Please let me go.'

'No!' said Helena. 'Don't open the door. We don't want the shop full of shirkers.'

Dinu said in Greek: 'As soon as the crowds have passed, I'll go with Xanthus.'

'Me too,' said Kid Plato. 'Democracy in action!'

I looked at Crina. 'We're going to the Pnyx to watch democracy in action.' Then I added in slow, simple Greek, 'Do you want to come with us?'

'*Panu gay!*' she cried. Certainly!

Simona said, 'I wish I could go too.'

'Why can't you?' I asked. 'Because of your eyes?'

'No! Because I'm a girl.'

'What did she just say?' Crina asked me. 'I missed a word.'

'She wants to go too, but she can't because she's a girl.'

Crina stared at me in disbelief.

I held up both hands. 'Don't blame me! It's ancient Athens.'

Crina turned to Simona and pointed at herself. 'Me girl!' she said in bad Greek. 'And me going!'

Simona and the other mini-cobblers all stared at her.

'You're a girl?'

'*Panu gay!*' Certainly! Then she mimed scissors and cutting her hair.

Simona squinted at her, going right up close. Then she turned and ran out of the courtyard and up a dark stairwell.

'Now look what you've done,' said Dinu.

Crina gave a snort of disgust. 'Some democracy! The only people allowed to vote are freeborn men.' She counted on her fingers. 'No women, no kids and don't even get me started on the fact that they have slaves.'

Kid Plato was watching her with his wise black eyes. Then he turned to me. 'What is she saying?'

I shrugged. 'She says you can't call it a democracy if only adult male citizens are allowed to vote.'

Kid Plato looked thoughtful. Then he said to Crina, 'You speak the truth, O maiden.'

Xanthus was twisting his hands together, 'Please can we go now? My master needs me.'

'How old are you, Xanthus?' I asked the boy.

'Thirteen summers.' he said.

I shuddered. He was the same age as me.

'Do you like your master?' I asked him.

'I love him,' declared Xanthus.

'I think it should be safe to go out now,' said Kid Plato. He took off his garland and gave it to one of the twins.

Dinu handed his garland to the other twin and Crina gave hers to Helena.

The twins lifted the crossbeam and let it slide onto the ground before propping it against the wall again. Then Helena pushed open one of the doors just far enough for us all to see that the road was empty again, apart from a stray dog sniffing the wall on the other side.

'It's safe,' said little Paulos confidently. 'Can I go too?'

Simona's voice from behind us said, 'Absolutely not! You stay here with Helena and the twins!'

'Simona!' cried Helena. 'What have you done?'

We all turned to see Simona with freshly chopped hair and wearing a boy's chiton.

'I've done the same thing she did!' Simona pointed at Crina then turned to her sister. 'Helena, once we've gone you must close the doors and bar them again. Remember what Father said: the shop is closed for the rest of the day.'

Helena merely nodded, a shocked expression still on her face.

The six of us went out onto the now deserted, furnace-hot road: Kid Plato, Dinu and Xanthus leading the way with me, Crina and Simona following behind.

Simona was squinting around happily, as if she had never been outside before.

The thought occurred to me that by inspiring Simona to take such drastic action, Crina had violated the third rule of time travel: *As little interaction as possible.*

'Watch out!' I grabbed Simona's arm just in time to save her from stepping in a steaming pile of mule dung.

'Thank you,' she said. I kept her arm linked in mine as Kid Plato had done with me earlier.

In front of us, some girls with jars on their heads emerged from between columns of a small building. I could hear splashing inside and realised that the building was a fountain house like on Greek vases my gran had shown me. The girls shot us shy glances but didn't seem to notice that two of our number were girls disguised as boys.

As we moved past the fountain house, the Acropolis came into view on our left.

'Look, Alexis,' said Simona. 'The Acropolis.'

'Can you see it?' I asked. I noticed her eyes seemed less

crossed than they had in the courtyard. Maybe looking at distant objects was good for her.

'Yes. I can see things far off or close up. It is middle distance that is difficult. I lived up on the Acropolis for nine months when I was seven,' she added.

'You lived there?'

'Yes. I was one of the girls chosen to weave a peplos for the goddess. They do it every four years.'

'Ah!' I said. 'For the Panathenaic festival.'

Up ahead Dinu had his head cocked to one side, just as Alcibiades did. The thought occurred to me that he could easily pass for Alcibiades' son. Simona was watching him and she must have had the same idea, because she turned to me and whispered. 'Alexis, you must tell your friend Dinu to beware of Alcibiades.'

'What do you mean?'

'You know what Alcibiades said about Socrates? That he is like an ugly Silenus with the beautiful god inside?'

'Yes?'

She brought her mouth very close to my ear. 'Alcibiades is the opposite. He is beautiful outside, but inside he is ugly.'

# 38
# The Storyteller

I 'll never forget my eighth birthday, because it was the last birthday when my parents were still alive.

At the time I was into dinosaurs and also Greek myths, so Mum made a cake that showed Hercules bashing a Tyrannosaurus rex with his club. Everyone got a badge with the name of a Greek god or goddess on it and also a plastic dinosaur to take home.

Anyway, the point of this story is Daniel the Storyteller. He was a friend of my dad's. He was trying to make it as an actor but in the meantime was doing kids' birthday parties.

I remember being upset because I had asked for a magician and when my dad said we were getting his friend Daniel I thought he would be rubbish. But he was amazing. He didn't have props or anything. Just his voice and his face and his body. When he started to tell the story everybody went absolutely quiet, even Callum Carter, who hardly ever sat still. Daniel told us the story of how Odysseus, the wiliest of the Greeks, killed all Penelope's suitors with his bow and arrows.

That was the day I put aside my dinosaurs to devote myself to ancient Greeks and Romans.

When Alcibiades got up to speak at the Assembly, he captivated the crowds just like Daniel the Storyteller.

First of all, he looked amazing. He was still wearing his long charioteer's tunic and the breeze blew it against his body so you could see how muscular he was. Second, he was one of the few people there with blond hair. The sun made it glint like gold. Third, even from a distance his gaze was piercing. When he turned your way, it felt as if he was speaking just to you. Then there was the way he moved his body and arms. It made you not want to look away. But the most impressive thing about him was the way he made his voice carry.

We kids had climbed a pine tree to see over the crowds. I reckoned there were five thousand men there at least.

Although the cicadas were chirping loudly around us, we could hear Alcibiades perfectly.

He made his listeners laugh, nod their heads in agreement and finally burst out in rapturous applause.

All except for Crina, Simona and Kid Plato.

'Wasn't he brilliant?' said Dinu in Greek.

'Amazing,' I replied in the same language.

But Crina whispered in English, 'He reminds me of all

those politicians who wave their arms a lot but are full of hot air.'

And Simona asked: 'What did he actually *say*?'

'He hardly even addressed the charge,' came the voice of Kid Plato from the lowest branch. 'He mainly talked about how he wins every contest he enters so they have to keep him on as general! And like a typical sophist, he won over the crowd.'

I told Crina what Kid Plato had said.

'Look!' cried Xanthus, as an official stepped forward. 'They're going to vote.'

Five thousand Athenians fell silent.

When the official asked how many people cast their vote to condemn Alcibiades, only a few hands went up.

When he asked how many of them wanted to pardon the general so that he could lead the fleet to Sicily, almost everyone raised an arm or a walking stick high in the air.

'Woohoo!' shouted Dinu and Xanthus cheered too.

But at the word 'Sicily' I felt a chill pass through my body and the pine tree started to tip strangely.

'Oh my God!' I gripped the branch and willed myself not to faint. 'It's the Expedition to Sicily!'

'What does that mean?' said Dinu. We were speaking in English.

'Everybody's been talking about Syracuse,' I said, 'which means nothing to me. But the herald just said Sicily.'

'Sicily?' said Crina. 'I read about that in one of my books.' Then she reached out and gripped my arm. 'Oh my God. Is that the guy who came up with the idea? I thought his name was Al Sibees!'

'Al-sib-EYE-uh-deez in English, but Al-kibee-AH-deez in Greek,' I said.

'Oh no!'

'What are you talking about?' Dinu pulled himself up and his face appeared below us, framed by pine needles.

I took a deep breath. 'Alcibiades has just convinced the Athenians to let him lead the fleet to Sicily in order to get their gold and then defeat the Spartans once and for all.'

'What's so terrible about that?' he said.

I took a deep breath. 'The Sicilian Expedition is destined to be the biggest military disaster in the history of Athens. It will ultimately cause her downfall.'

Dinu was looking at me with wide eyes.

I leaned closer to him. Even though we were speaking English I lowered my voice. 'Don't you remember? Magister Gerardus wrote the figures on the whiteboard. The Athenians will lose two hundred ships and twenty thousand men will die.'

'Oh my God!' breathed Crina. 'Twenty thousand men!'

'I've got to warn him!' said Dinu suddenly. The branches of the pine sprang back as he started to climb down out of the tree.

'Dinu!' I cried as he landed in a puff of dust. 'Don't tell him! It's one of the biggest disasters in the history of the world. If you stop him, you'll definitely change the future!'

But I was too late; Dinu was already running down the dusty slope of the Pnyx.

# 39

# Wild Chicken Chase

What would you do if you knew you could stop thousands of people dying, but by doing so you would create a future that did not contain your friends or family? And knowing that you yourself would also vanish in a puff?

Solomon Daisy had warned us that changing major – or even minor – historical events could have far-reaching and unthinkable consequences. That was why he had given us the third rule of time travel: *As little interaction as possible.*

If Dinu reached Alcibiades and convinced him not to go to Sicily, the three of us would certainly vanish, because history would have been changed forever.

Crina and I jumped out of the tree and, without even a backwards glance at Kid Plato or Simona, we pelted after Dinu.

Luckily there were five thousand citizens – that is, freeborn men over the age of eighteen – between Dinu and Alcibiades.

Luckily Dinu's blond hair stood out among all those dark heads.

Unluckily he was heading back to the Agora with thousands of others. Crina and I lost sight of him somewhere between the South Stoa and the mint, the same buildings I had glimpsed shortly after landing the night before.

The Agora was already full of chattering groups of men, each with an opinion on Alcibiades and his virtues and vices.

'Where did he go?' gasped Crina. 'Alex, we have to find him or he'll change the future!'

I nodded, out of breath. 'And the moment . . . he changes the future . . . we'll be dead.'

'There!' She pointed towards the north. 'Look – he's going that way, moving fast.'

We ran past now-familiar stalls and altars and finally emerged at the Herms crossroad. I recognised the Painted Stoa, where I had first seen Socrates and found Crina.

'Now where?' I panted.

'There! See his blond head? Going into that big arch!' Crina pointed west towards a monumental gate. 'Is that the Dipylon Gate?' she asked me.

'I think so. But how do you know?'

*'Athens on Five Drachmas a Day,* of course!'

We must have left the boundary of the Agora because now I saw women washing clothes in some kind of stream on our left. I realised it was the channelled Eridanus river. On the right-hand side of the road other women stood at tall looms, weaving bright cloth. They were unveiled and some wore lots of make-up.

Crina and I gratefully reached the shade of the massive gate, with its high, vaulted roof. I thought I saw the glint of Dinu's yellow hair up ahead too, so we hurried on, passing under another big arch and back out into blazing sunshine. Now we were in the graveyard among the tombs, for we were outside the town walls. A few dozen men were hurrying along the road, presumably on their way home to tell their families about the Assembly. Most of them were making their way on foot, but one guy rode a small but fast-moving donkey.

He was wearing a straw hat.

A yellow, brimless straw hat that looked just like blond hair.

'Oh no!' Crina gasped. 'I took us on a wild chicken chase. I feel so stupid.'

'Don't feel stupid.' I rested my hands on my knees to catch my breath. 'I thought it was him too. Maybe it will be all right. Maybe Dinu will decide *not* to tell Alcibiades something that will change the course of history.'

Crina merely raised an eyebrow and I had to laugh.

'Prepare to go *kerpluff*,' I said, only half joking. 'But seriously, we'd better find him.'

Still breathing hard from all the running, we turned and headed back towards the big Dipylon Gate in silence.

Suddenly Crina stopped. 'Alex, listen.'

'What? Do you hear Dinu? Or Alcibiades?'

'No. I hear nature.'

She was right. It wasn't silent at all. In addition to the rhythmic chirp of the cicadas, the air was full of the sounds of insects and birds.

'Alex, when was the last time you heard a bird sing in London?'

I shrugged. 'Ducks on the river?' I said. 'Pigeons on the pavement?'

She touched my arm. 'Listen! What's that one called?'

'Dunno. My mum used to call them "twig birds". You know: little birds that hop about on twigs?'

Crina cocked her head. 'I know that purring one is a turtle dove . . . and the one up high is a skylark. And the bees! Can you hear the bees buzzing?'

'Yes, I can hear the birds and the bees.' I waggled my eyebrows at her but she didn't notice.

She was pointing at something moving by the side of the road. An old tortoise pushed through the wildflowers and weeds at the foot of painted tombs. A small rodent – possibly a shrew – skittered across the road.

I could smell green leaves cooking in the sun and sweet flowers and the faint turpentine scent of pine.

Perhaps because we could be snuffed out of existence at any moment, the world had never seemed so full of life.

'It is amazing,' I said.

Crina nodded. 'This is what the world is supposed to be like. Full of birds and insects and plants and creatures. It's like this in my grandmother's village in Romania. There's so much life. England could be like this too.'

'Is that why you go on all those marches and wear your eco T-shirts and stuff?' I said.

'Yes. We need to do everything we can to save the world – if it's not already too late.'

As we left the road and wandered among the tombs, Crina asked me the names of the flowers and plants we could see.

'Those little yellow ones are buttercups,' I said. 'And there are some red poppies. We have those in England too. But I don't know that white and purple one. Or the one with spiky leaves.'

A white butterfly did lazy loops through the shimmering heat of the afternoon.

'Did you know that the Greek word for butterfly also means "soul"?' I said. '*Psyche*.'

'That's beautiful,' she said, and after a pause, 'Alex, do you believe in the soul? I mean, like Socrates does? As a part of you that will never die but will fly off into the air?'

'Until last night I wasn't sure,' I said. 'But after I inhaled the incense and listened to the gong, something inside me floated up and I could see myself from above.'

'That happened to me once when I was little,' she said. 'I remember watching my grandmother's goat give birth. In my memory of it, I can see myself.'

And then she said something that took me by surprise.

'Alex?'

'Yes?'

'Tell me about Plecta?'

# 40
# Soul Butterflies

Plecta was a girl I had met in Roman London.

Even though I only knew her for a few hours I had loved her.

I kicked a pebble and watched it disappear among the wildflowers at the base of a column tomb. 'You've read my diary. What else do you want to know?'

Out of the corner of my eye I saw Crina looking at me. 'Did you really love her? It wasn't just Tittles? You know, Time Travellers' Love Syndrome.'

Another butterfly swam dizzily past the painted grave markers.

'I've been thinking about that a lot,' I said. 'I think it was real. Did you understand Socrates earlier at Simon's, when he was going on about how the soul is the most important part of us and how we should keep it pure by doing what is right?'

'A little bit. But I've read about that too.'

'Well, I know it sounds cheesy, but Plecta had a really beautiful soul. It shone out of her and made her beautiful.'

I glanced at Crina. Her head was down, but I could see her cheeks were flushed.

I took a deep breath. 'Kind of like you,' I said.

Her head came up and she looked at me. Up close I could see her brown eyes weren't brown at all but grey with flecks of blue and yellow.

'You think I have a beautiful soul?'

I didn't trust my voice so I just nodded.

Her face was flushed. 'God, this heat,' she said shyly.

'I know.' I gave a nervous laugh. 'My throat is as parched as a sock fresh from the tumble dryer.'

'Look! That must be the Sacred Gate. And it has a fountain!'

We had emerged from the tombs onto a broad road leading to a slightly smaller version of the Dipylon Gate. Sure enough, I spotted a marble fountain beside the arched entrance.

When we reached it, Crina hesitated. 'Is it safe to drink?'

'Let me test it,' I said. 'I've already drunk from a fountain in the harbour.' I took a sip then drank deeply then plunged my whole head into the basin.

'That is so good!' I said when I came up for air.

Crina also drank and immersed her head. When she rose

up again there were tiny beads of water sparkling on the tips of her eyelashes.

As we moved into the big cool space of the Sacred Gate I saw about two dozen potters' stalls selling everything from tiny votive figures to big kraters: the mixing bowls for wine.

'Look, Alex, this must be the potters' district.'

'Yeah,' I said. 'I always imagined it outdoors like in *Ancient Greek Assassins*, but it's much nicer here in the shade.'

But when we left the relative cool of the covered gate for the blast furnace of the afternoon, I noticed there were potters here too. A whole street of them, in fact. They were mainly tanned young men in linen loincloths. Some were stamping clay in watery pits. Some sat on the ground, spinning the potters' wheels on which their masters shaped the vases. A few sat in the tiger-striped shade of split-reed awnings, delicately painting unfired pots. I could see black smoke from the kilns rising up from behind the white cube buildings.

'I love Greek vases,' said Crina.

'You do? How do you even know about them?'

'I found a lot on the Internet when I was prepping for this trip. The pictures on them are like graphic novels.'

'I know!' I said. 'My gran says the vase-painters of Athens were geniuses on a level with Picasso.'

'If Picasso had illustrated comic books,' said Crina.

I stared at Crina. The last hour had been a revelation.

'Look!' Crina pointed. 'A girl potter!'

We stopped for a moment to watch a skinny girl with pinned-up black hair painting a big pot on an upturned basket before her.

'See?' I said. 'Maybe ancient Athens isn't so bad after all.'

'She's probably a slave,' muttered Crina. 'Shall we go ask?'

'I think we'd be better off running,' I said. 'It's our friends from last night.'

'What?'

Silently I pointed to the two archers. I recognised one of them from the night before.

And Archer Two recognised me.

'There they are!' He notched an arrow. 'Xtop them!'

# 41
# Water Nymphs

We ran.

Without thinking I grabbed Crina's hand just like Finn grabs Rey's hand in *Star Wars: The Force Awakens*.

Unlike Rey, she did not let go.

'How do you know where you're going?' she cried, as I pulled her off the Street of the Potters down a shadowed, stinking alley.

'I don't!' I gasped. 'But if I can just keep the Acropolis in sight I'll know roughly where we are.'

A few moments later the Acropolis disappeared behind a hill.

'Sod's law,' I muttered to myself.

We carried on running, past feta-cube houses, with a hill rising behind them on the left and the city wall on our right. Perched on top of the hill, I saw trees and between them the columns of a temple. Not the Parthenon but the Temple of

Hephaestus, where the metal workers had their stalls.

'I think that's the Market Hill!' I glanced over my shoulder and saw the floppy Smurf hats still on our trail.

I pulled Crina down a street of sawing, hammering carpenters, then right down another alley, then left along the city wall again.

Turning onto one road, we saw a herd of pigs coming our way. They were big – proper hogs – and they filled the whole street from one side to the other, squealing and grunting and jostling each other. If we hadn't dived into an alleyway between two houses, we would have been driven back towards our pursuers.

Then I caught sight of the Acropolis above a red-tiled roof and I knew which way to go.

Heading towards it, we came into a street full of the clinking of metal chisels on stone: the Street of the Marble Workers. At the crossroads stood the State Prison.

'I know where we are!' I cried. 'Simon's house is just up ahead.'

'Wait!' Crina grabbed my arm. 'We can't go straight there, in case the guards are still following us! If they find out that Simon offered us shelter, then he and his children might get in trouble.'

'What do you suggest?'

'Hide somewhere to see if they're still on our trail!'

'Good idea. But where?'

'There!' Crina pointed at two girls coming out of the fountain house we had passed earlier. This time she was the one who took my hand. She pulled me up the street to a little red-roofed building on our right.

Plunging between two columns, we found ourselves in a cool, dim space with the echoing sounds of girls' singing above the splash of water and the gurgle of drains.

The two girls fell silent a moment after we entered. They held water jars on the edge of a marble trough, tilted to catch the water gushing out of lion-head spouts in the wall. They glanced at each other and then giggled.

'*Chairete!*' I panted. Greetings. Then I turned and peered out from behind one of the columns.

'Can you see them?' whispered Crina in my ear.

'No, I think we're safe. Oh, wait!' I leaned out a little further. 'Uh-oh! They're coming this way. And they're stopping to look in all the shops.'

I turned and looked around the dimly lit space with its wobbling rings of light on the ceiling. The two fountain basins, one on each side, were about the size of coffins. That gave me an idea. 'Please!' I said to the girls. 'Guards are searching for us, but we are innocent. Help us hide?'

After another shared glance the girls giggled and inclined their heads for 'yes'.

'Touch our heads when they come?' I said. Again they tipped their heads.

'You get into that basin, Crina!' I pointed. 'I'll get into this one. If the girl touches your head, go under and hold your breath as long as you can.'

She looked at me, wide-eyed. Then she nodded and jumped boldly into one of the troughs.

I jumped into the other.

I would have squealed, but the icy chill of the water had taken my breath away. I ducked under, and resurfaced dripping and gasping.

One of the girls had come over to my trough.

She smiled sweetly. Then she emptied her jar over me. 'What the . . . ?' I muttered. Then I understood. She needed the jar to be empty for when the guards came.

As she repositioned her water jar, I grinned with chattering teeth and nodded my thanks.

In the trough opposite I saw Crina's dripping head rise up. She gave me a wobbly smile and a thumbs-up.

Then the two girls did a clever thing: they resumed singing.

It was a song about a girl going to the well. The chorus was something to do with Artemis.

It seemed like ages. My arms and legs were starting to go numb. Then my girl widened her eyes and patted my head with her free hand. I knew what that meant.

The archers were here.

I took a deep breath, held my nose and sank as deep into the chilly water as I could.

# 42
# How to Save the World

They say a plunge in icy water is good for your muscles after a long run. They say it also boosts your immune system. They say that a dunking in cold water can even give you a feeling of euphoria, which comes from the Greek word for blissful happiness.

As Crina and I stood outside Simon the Shoemaker's house, already dry in the oven-hot heat, I was experiencing a weird mixture of euphoria and terror.

The euphoria came from the cold-water dousing and having escaped the guards.

The terror came from the knowledge that at any moment somewhere in the city Dinu might find Alcibiades and warn him not to go on the Sicilian Expedition, thereby saving thousands of Greek lives and changing the future forever so that the three of us time travellers would suddenly go *kerpluff*.

From inside the house, we could hear Simon's angry voice.

'What were you thinking? Isn't it enough that I allow you to help me make shoes instead of weaving at the loom? Isn't it enough that you have responsibility when I'm not here?'

'But, Father,' came Simona's muffled voice, 'I was just showing hospitality to our guest-friends. One of them was a girl pretending to be a boy. That's what gave me the idea.'

'A girl? I don't believe it!'

I looked at Crina. 'Now is our moment. Trust me.'

I knocked on the right-hand door and a moment later it opened to Simon's angry face.

'We're sorry we caused trouble for your daughter,' I said. 'She was only showing us kindness.'

Simon glared at me from under his black eyebrow. 'Do you know the guards were here a short time ago, looking for two boys who robbed the goddess and profaned the Mysteries?'

'What did you tell them?'

'Nothing. Because you are friends of Socrates.' He turned his fierce glare on Crina. 'Is it true that you are a girl?'

Crina understood and tipped her head for yes.

'Your elders allow you to dress as a boy?'

I said, 'Please, sir, Crina only dressed like a boy because she was lost and desperate to find us. Socrates and his wife helped her.'

Simon's scowl turned to a frown. 'Socrates and Xanthippe helped her do this?'

'Yes,' I said. 'And now our friend Dinu is missing. Please

196

will you help us find him so we can go home? That's all we want,' I added. 'To go home.'

His expression softened a little. 'You'd better come in,' he said gruffly and stood aside for us to enter. 'I don't know where your friend is. But I will go into the Agora and ask. Allophanes, the sausage-seller, always knows everything. Simona!' he cried over his shoulder. 'Come look after our guests and make sure your brothers and sister stay upstairs.'

Simona stepped out of a doorway. 'Yes, Father,' she said meekly.

Her father took one of the walking sticks leaning against the wall and went out.

'Tell Simona I'm sorry for getting her in trouble,' said Crina.

I told Simona how Crina felt.

'Don't be sorry!' Simona hurried forward and grasped Crina's hands. 'Apart from when I brought the peplos to Athena, it was the most wonderful afternoon of my life. To be outside. To see all those people . . . I loved it. And I love the way my head feels so light and cool.' She touched her dark curls.

'Simona,' I said, 'earlier you told us Alcibiades was ugly inside. Do you really believe that?'

'Yes. Because he is beautiful, many people admire him and think his soul must be beautiful. But it is rotten. A few years ago someone dared him to hit a man he hardly knew, a friend of my father's. And he did it. Just to win a wager. He punched him with his fist and Hipponicus lost a tooth.'

I told Crina what Simona had said.

'You speak the truth?' asked Crina, making her memorised phrase into a question.

'I speak the truth.' Simona's face was grim. 'Then two years ago Alcibiades bought a beautiful dog of the sort famous for their silky tails. His dog had the longest, silkiest tail of all. When everyone kept going on about how beautiful the dog's tail was, he took an axe and chopped it off.'

When I told Crina this, her eyes filled with angry tears.

'People were appalled,' continued Simona, 'but Alcibiades just laughed and said that was what he wanted: for all of Athens to be talking about him.'

At that moment the front door swung open and Simon came in, sweaty but smiling. 'Good news!' He leaned his walking stick against the wall by the door. 'Your friend was training with Alcibiades at the palaestra.'

'Did you see them? Did you talk to him? Did you beg him to come back here?'

'They'd just left when I got there, but Alcibiades is attending a symposium this evening. I imagine your friend will go with him.'

'St Nektarios be praised!' I breathed a sigh of relief and said to Crina, 'Dinu is with Alcibiades, but he must not have warned him yet. They're going to a symposium this evening.'

'What's a symposium?'

'It's an after-dinner party where men drink wine together.'

'Oh yes! I read about those. They could be very tame or really rowdy, depending on the host.'

'Exactly.' I turned to Simon. 'Do you know who's hosting the party?'

'A rich young man named Euphiletus.'

'Can you please take us?' I asked Simon. 'So that we can get Dinu and return to our own land.'

'I'm afraid I can't. I myself have been invited to a symposium a few miles outside the city walls so I must set out now. But the house of Euphiletus is easy enough to find. It's at the foot of the Acropolis, on the south side. The porch has red-and-white striped columns. Anyone can point the way.'

'Father, may Alex and Crina rest here until it's time for them to go?' Simona asked. 'They're very tired and can have a short nap.'

'Very well, but make sure your brothers and sister stay upstairs.'

'Thank you, Father.'

'Thank you, sir,' I echoed. 'We are grateful for your help.'

Simona unrolled two rush mats for us to lie on right there in the courtyard. Crina and I stretched out next to each other, and I closed my eyes. But my heart was still thudding and my mind was racing.

If Dinu had found Alcibiades and we were still alive, that meant he hadn't yet told him anything that would affect the future. But knowing Dinu, he could let something slip at any moment.

I looked up at the grapevine ceiling. The late-afternoon sun made the leaves glow like emeralds.

'Please, God,' I prayed in my mind, 'may Dinu keep his mouth shut until we get to him. And please may he come home with us. I promise I'll never time travel again.'

I must have slept because Simona's whisper woke me: 'Alexis! Wake up!'

The cooler temperature and the light in the courtyard told me that a few hours had passed.

I sat up groggily to see Simona's squinting face up close to mine. She sat back and I saw Crina sitting cross-legged on a mat, twirling something like a spinning top with wool coming out.

I yawned. 'What's that?' I spoke in English without thinking.

'A spindle,' said Crina, 'for making wool into yarn that can be woven.'

'So we're still alive?'

She put the spindle and wool into a basket and nodded.

I looked at Simona, who was sitting back on her heels.

'Is it time to go to the symposium?'

'Yes, but I've been thinking about it. There's a problem. I tried to explain to your friend but she didn't understand.'

I rubbed my eyes. 'A problem?'

'Yes. They might not let you in. Children don't usually attend those kinds of parties. Unless they're entertainers.'

'We can wait outside until Dinu arrives with Alcibiades.'

'But it might be dangerous to wait on the street outside. The archers are looking for you, correct?'

'Yes. But what else can we do?'

'I've got an idea, but I'm not sure if it will work. I don't suppose either of you can play the aulos?' said Simona. She held out two thin bone recorders with reed mouthpieces. They were like the ones Alcibiades' flute-girls had been playing the night before. To our surprise, she put them both in her mouth and her cheeks puffed out as she played a buzzy tune.

When she stopped we both clapped and she flushed with pleasure.

'Crina plays an instrument called a clarinet,' I said, 'which has a reed like those. And I play something called a recorder, with the same kind of holes, so, yes – we both can.'

Simona rose to her feet and held out a hand to help me up. 'Then I think I know how I can get you into the party!'

# 43
# Swing Low

If you had been a hawk soaring over Athens that evening you would have seen a dark-haired youth with a walking stick leading two saffron-veiled flute-girls through the narrow streets of Athens, heading towards the south side of the Acropolis. If you had swooped down a little lower you might have noticed that the flute-girls had short hair under their veils, and might actually be flute-boys. If you had perched on the edge of a red-tiled roof and used your keen vision to scrutinise their faces, you would still be confused. Were they boys? Were they girls?

The sun had set and the air was cooler, but it was still warm. A faint breeze ruffled our headscarves and cooled me as it dried the sheen of sweat on my face. I could smell woodsmoke, animal dung and somewhere the whiff of sizzling sausage.

Crina was playing as we walked, working out a jazzy version of 'Twinkle, Twinkle, Little Star' on Simona's aulos.

Because she was better at playing it, I had been given a pair of little bronze finger-cymbals to keep the beat.

We turned a corner guarded by a very masculine herm and Simona pointed out a house a few metres along with two red-and-white striped columns flanking dark blue double doors.

I stopped dinging my cymbals. 'That must be it,' I said to Crina, who had also stopped playing.

'It looks like the American flag!' she murmured.

'This is the house of Euphiletus,' said Simona, stopping outside. 'If my plan works, then I'll have to bid you farewell now.'

'Thank you for all your help,' I said, and clasped her hand in gratitude.

Crina stepped forward. 'Thank you, Simona,' she said in Greek, and gave the girl a quick hug.

Simona had borrowed one of her dad's walking sticks. She now used this to rap on the front door.

A moment later the door opened a crack. 'Password?' said a voice from inside.

'Flute-girls for Alcibiades,' said Simona.

'That's not the password.' Pause. 'But it will do.'

The doors swung open.

Crina and I gave Simona a final quick wave.

'You opened my eyes,' were her last words. 'I will never forget you.'

Crina and I stepped over the threshold and into a beautiful tiled courtyard with two palm trees reaching up into the lemon-yellow sky of dusk.

The doorkeeper was a bald man with puffy eyes, wearing a long chiton. He pointed towards a bent-over slave with a couch on his back just disappearing into a room across the courtyard.

'Follow that slave into the *andron*,' he commanded.

The dining room was full of the sound of men's voices, the heat of their bodies and the smell of perfume and sweat.

As my eyes adjusted to the dim light, I saw over a dozen men reclining in pairs on seven high couches. Each man had at least one slave in attendance. Some were standing or sitting, but a few crouched under their master's couch.

On the central couch against the far wall I saw Dinu reclining in front of Alcibiades. Xanthus the slave boy was almost invisible in the shadows beneath.

When Dinu spotted us, his eyes widened.

He grinned and waved but didn't get up. Alcibiades, on the other hand, gracefully slipped off the back of the couch and came forward with his head cocked to one side as usual. 'Alexis! Crina!' he lisped. 'How delightful that you have come to play for us. This is our host, Euphiletus.'

He put his arm around a beardless youth with dark hair and the longest eyelashes I have ever seen on a guy.

'Welcome,' said Eyelashes. 'Any friend of the general is

a friend of mine.'

'We've come to fetch Dinu,' I said. 'We've received word from home. He's needed urgently.' I turned to Dinu. 'Come on!' I whispered in English. 'We've accomplished the mission. Let's go home.'

'Before you do anything to change the future!' added Crina.

'What's the rush?' said Dinu in Greek. 'We don't need to leave until an hour before midnight.'

Alcibiades clapped his hands. 'Then we have hours and hours! You must stay and play for us. But first have some food! There are jellied eels, pickled quail eggs and roasted thrush.'

Crina recoiled from the bowls of slimy eels, tiny hard-boiled eggs and whole roasted birds the size of my thumb.

'We're not hungry,' I said quickly.

'Then play a song! Play us something from your faraway land!'

I glanced at Crina and nodded. At least if we were here we would be able to stop Dinu from blurting out something that might prove fatal.

Alcibiades climbed back onto the couch behind Dinu and gestured for us to begin.

Crina sucked the two reeds of the aulos to wet them.

Then she inclined her head towards me. 'The last song I learned was "Swing Low, Sweet Chariot". Do you know the words?'

'Yes,' I said. 'I sang it at a talent show at my primary school. Play it real slow to make it last.'

Crina's cheeks puffed out as she started to play her buzzy aulos.

'*Swing low, sweet chariot,*' I sang in my nice high choirboy's voice. '*Coming for to carry me home . . .*'

Chipmunk-cheeked Crina turned wide-eyed to look at me and raised her eyebrows as if to say 'Wow!'

I carried on singing, and I also kept time by chiming my bronze finger-cymbals together. '*I looked over Jordan* (ding!), *and what did I see* (ding!), *coming for to carry me home?* (Ding, ding!) *A band of angels* (ding!), *coming after me* (ding!), *coming for to carry me home.*'

The chatter in the room died down as some of the reclining diners stopped to listen.

I sang the chorus a little softer, so as not to drown out the buzzy aulos.

But that made everybody even quieter.

'*If you get there before I do (Coming for to carry me home), tell all of my friends that I'm coming there too (Coming for to carry me home).*'

Now all the men were silent. One or two had actually paused with food halfway to their mouths.

'*Sometimes I'm up, sometimes I'm down (Coming for to carry me home), but still my soul feels heavenly bound (Coming for to carry me home).*'

After the final chorus, I stopped singing and Crina lowered her aulos.

For a moment there was absolute silence.

Then the room erupted in applause.

'That was sublime,' called Eyelashes from against the far wall. 'What is the song about?'

'It's about a chariot coming to carry your soul to heaven after you die.'

'Is it a song of the Mysteries? Or one about the soul?' lisped Alcibiades. 'Either way, I approve. Play it again!'

Each time we played it, the men clapped harder and harder. I could almost feel waves of adoration. Crina must have felt the same way. Her eyes were bright.

After the fifth reprise Alcibiades cocked his head. 'Beautiful. But what else do you have for us?'

I looked at Crina. 'Do you know "King of the Swingers"?' I whispered.

She raised her eyebrows at me. 'Or how about Bluzie's song: *Take me back, Alex . . . I'll go anywhere with you . . .*'

# 44

# Throwing Wine

Dusk turned to night as Crina and I entertained the symposiasts with music.

'King of the Swingers' went down a treat.

So did 'Take Me Back', 'Greensleeves' and 'Twinkle, Twinkle, Little Star'. The last song was appropriate as some of the house slaves brought in bronze oil lamps on stands to fill the room with flickering light and smoke.

The men had now finished eating so the slaves took away the small tables with the remains of the food and came back in with flat drinking cups and garlands, one for each diner.

You'd think a wreath of ivy, violets and daisies on a man's head would look girlish but somehow it worked. It made them look like commandos in a jungle.

Meanwhile, two other house slaves brought in some pots and set them on the floor in the middle of the room. The biggest was a krater, the ancient version of a punchbowl and twice as big as the one we had seen at Simon the Shoemaker's. It was big enough to bathe a baby in, though the baby would have got very drunk, for it was full of wine.

Eyelashes got down from his couch and stood over the slaves so he could tell them how much water to add.

Then he gestured for all the slaves to leave.

Without them, the room suddenly seemed different. Empty and flickering and mysterious.

'This is when the drinking portion of the banquet begins,' I whispered to Crina. 'The proper symposium.'

'Perhaps our singer would like to serve the wine?' Alcibiades was looking at me, his eyes glowing green in the yellow lamplight. 'It is a great honour to do so,' he added in his charming lisp.

'He wants me to be the wine-server,' I whispered to Crina.

'Better you than me,' she murmured. 'I'll just sit in the shadows and keep an eye on Dinu.'

I started towards the krater, but Eyelashes stopped me with a gesture. He uttered a prayer, poured a libation of wine on the packed clay floor, and led the men in a short hymn to the gods.

Finally, he beckoned me over.

'Have you done this before?'

'No,' I confessed.

'Just dip this jug in the krater, go around and fill each man's kylix with wine. Make sure nobody's cup goes dry!'

As I went round I noticed there was a different design inside each man's cup. It was on the bottom, so it would only be revealed when they had drained the contents. When I got to Dinu I whispered, 'Go easy. We have four more hours before midnight.' His cup had a Medusa sticking her tongue out.

He ignored me and took a big swig. Immediately he choked and had to be patted on the back by a laughing Alcibiades.

I topped Dinu up a little, warning him in English, 'Make that last all evening or Medusa will turn you to stone.'

'Speech! Speech!' cried Eyelashes. 'I call for a speech from each of you in praise of Alcibiades, our guest of honour!'

Each of the guests said something nice about the general. One praised his wealth, another his good looks and another his boldness.

One young man with straight black hair produced a lyre from beneath his couch and sang what he called an 'Ode to Alcibiades'.

In between keeping their cups filled, I found a spare cup and filled it with well-watered wine for Crina, who sat in the shadows at the foot of a couch. Every so often I took a sip too.

By the time each man had made a speech, they were pretty tipsy and the big krater of wine was almost empty, with nothing but dark red sludge at the bottom.

Eyelashes came over and peered into the ancient punchbowl. 'Fill their cups with the dregs,' he said, 'so we can play *kottabos*.'

He opened the door and spoke to someone out in the courtyard. A few moments later a slave came in with a tall thin rod on a base and a little bronze bowl.

I scooped up as much of the dregs as I could in my wine-pouring jug and as I went around the guests giving them each a dribble of blood-red gloop, the slave set up the rod in the middle of the krater. Then he balanced the small bronze bowl on top.

I went over to Crina. 'It's for a game called *kottabos*!' I told her. 'I've seen it painted on ancient pots in the British Museum. Have you heard of it?'

'No. Tell me.'

'The aim is to knock the bowl off the stand. If you succeed, then the gods grant your wish.' I tipped my head towards a diner with a little goatee beard. 'That guy just prayed that his pregnant wife will give birth to a boy. Now watch. He's going to throw.' Goat Beard pushed himself higher on his left elbow, hooked his forefinger in one of the little handles of the kylix and flicked his wine dregs at the copper bowl.

The dregs splattered harmlessly on the wall behind and everyone laughed.

'May Philippos return my affections upon my return,' cried the second diner, who looked like a rugby player. Everyone laughed again as he missed too.

'May Alcibiades return my affections tonight,' cried the youth with the lyre, and everybody laughed before he had even made his throw.

All the other guests took it in turn to flick their last bit of muddy wine at the bowl, at the same time calling out a wish.

Dinu was last. So far nobody had knocked the bowl from its stand. 'It's down to you,' I heard Alcibiades tell him. 'Otherwise it's bad luck for us all.'

The flickering yellow flame of an oil lamp made Dinu's leafy garland glow and turned his blue eyes green, so that he looked like a leopard in the jungle.

'Oh no!' Crina was getting to her feet. 'I know that look! He's going to do something stupid!'

But it was too late.

Dinu had already hooked his forefinger around the handle of the cup. As he flicked his kylix forward, he cried out in excellent Greek: 'May Alcibiades *not* take the expedition to Sicily!'

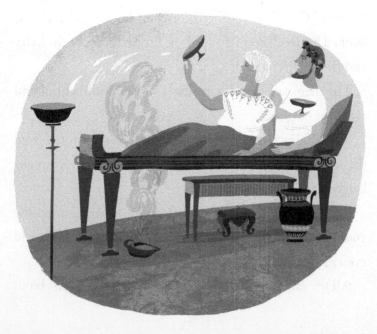

# 45
# Slip of the Tongue

I gasped. Dinu had done it. He had openly broken rule number three: *As little interaction as possible.*

I braced myself for oblivion.

Instead came the ominous clatter of bronze on packed earth.

Not only had Dinu wished the worst thing possible, but the gods seemed to have heard his prayer.

His glob of purple wine dregs had knocked the bowl off its perch.

It had fallen onto its rim and now wobbled in a circle on the floor, making a ringing sound as it came to rest.

The note of the ancient singing bowl died away, leaving the room in deathly silence.

Because Dinu was reclining in front of Alcibiades with his back to him, he didn't see the expression that flitted across his idol's face.

But I did.

It was fear.

'Dinu!' I hissed in English. 'Don't say another word!'

The other diners gaped at Dinu.

For a terrible moment I thought they might leap off their couches and attack him.

Then the good-looking youth who had played the lyre sat up straight on his couch. 'Did you hear what happened last month at Delphi?' he said in a quiet voice. 'Carrion crows attacked the gold statue of Athena.'

Another guest, a man who blinked constantly, said, 'When my wife drew water this morning, it was the colour of blood.'

'You know we're all willing to follow you to our graves,' said an older man who looked just like Stavros the limo-driver, 'but what if this is not the time to attack Sicily? What if the gods are sending us a warning?'

'Yes!' said the oldest guest of all, a man with two streaks of grey hair over his ears like a badger. 'What if the gods are warning us against hubris? We have only ever fought to defend ourselves. Never have we been the unprovoked aggressor.'

Alcibiades pinched the top of his nose and closed his eyes. 'I, too, have been having second thoughts,' he confessed. Then the violets in his garland trembled as he shook his head decisively. 'But it's too late. How can we stop the expedition now?'

'What if the people of Athens knew about the bad omens?'

said Rugby Player. 'Wouldn't they vote to abandon the whole enterprise? Isn't it our duty to tell them?'

'What?' said Badger Hair. 'Shall we gossip like old ladies? Telling them this bad dream or that possible portent?'

'We need to do something across the city,' cried Eyelashes, our host. 'And we need to do it tonight!'

'Yes!' agreed Stavros Lookalike. 'If the citizens see some kind of ill-omened sign they can take another vote.'

'A referendum!' said Rugby Player. 'In order to rectify the first vote.'

'Oh no!' I said to Crina. 'I wonder if this is when they smash the herms!'

I said it in English but in my utter stupidity I forgot that the word is the same in both languages.

'Herms?' cried Eyelashes, whose hearing must have been as sharp as a bat's. 'Do something to the herms, did you say?'

'They guard our passage around the city,' mused Lyre Guy, 'but also in and out of it.'

'And they stand for democracy,' said Blinker. 'What with their great variety of faces and their appeal to *hoi polloi*.'

'What if the herms could help us send a warning?' said a man with a pock-marked face.

'We could take off their garlands?' suggested Goat Beard.

'Something more drastic is needed,' said Rugby Player. 'We should smash them!'

'That's it!' cried Alcibiades. 'We'll smash the herms! Nicias is so superstitious that he'll call off the expedition for sure.'

'What?' Badger Hair's face was almost as white as the streaks in his hair. 'Deface the gods who protect our journeys, including our path to the underworld? Never!'

'I agree,' said Lyre Guy. 'That's too much. It would be an unheard-of sacrilege – worse than profaning the Mysteries.'

'And what if we are caught in the act?' cried Blinker.

'If we cover our faces, spread out and do it in the next hour, then we should be fine,' said Alcibiades. 'My years on the field have taught me to act decisively.' In spite of his lisp he sounded full of authority.

'My father is a stonemason,' said Rugby Player. 'He lives not far from here. He has hammers and chisels, and pieces of soft leather to muffle the noise.'

'Won't your father be ashamed of your cowardice?' cried Badger Hair.

'No!' said Rugby Player. 'He's been begging me not to go on the expedition. In fact, he'll probably join us!'

He slid off his couch and hurried out of the *andron*.

'What's happening?' Crina said in my ear.

I told her.

'Oh no, Alex!' She gripped my arm. 'You gave them the idea!'

I felt dizzy. Had I just done what I'd begged Dinu not to? Had I broken rule number three of time travel?

'Wait!' I said. 'I think it's OK. I'm not actually changing

anything. It's historical fact that someone smashed the herms . . .'

She frowned and shook her head. 'But, Alex, *you* gave them the idea!'

Angrily I shook off her arm. 'If I hadn't, then someone else would have. It was destined to happen.'

Alcibiades stood up and began to use all his skills of rhetoric to persuade Badger Hair, Lyre Guy and the other reluctant guests to join them.

He said it was for the good of Athens.

He said thousands of lives might be saved if we waited.

He said the gods would understand.

I don't remember everything else he said, only that by the end of his speech my heart was pounding with excitement.

As this was going to happen anyway, we might as well have some fun.

By the time Rugby Player and his dad arrived with a load of chisels and hammers and leather shammy cloths, almost everyone was up for the deed.

'Let's vote on it,' cried Eyelashes. 'Who's for smashing the herms around the city?'

Out of sixteen right hands, twelve went up.

One of them was Dinu's.

And one of them was mine.

# 46

# Herm Busters

When I was about seven, still living in Fulham with my parents, I saw my friend Callum steal some sweets from the corner shop. He said he did it all the time and never got caught.

I thought what Callum did was exciting.

I thought it would be cool to do something naughty. Just like Callum.

So I decided to break something.

Early one Sunday morning, before my parents were up, I took an empty jar out to the street. I looked right and left, but nobody was around. Heart pounding, I threw the jar onto the street.

It bounced.

After two more goes, it finally shattered in a satisfying explosion of shards.

Smashing the herms was a bit like that.

It felt bad and good at the same time.

Plus, there was a gang of us.

We all crowded out through the double front doors into the moonlit street. Eyelashes stopped by the herm on the corner, a few paces from his porch.

'We'll start with our herm!' he said. 'It's been here since before the Persians.' He turned to Rugby Player's dad, the stonemason. 'Show me how.'

'Place the shammy like this.' Stonemason Dad laid a soft piece of leather over the herm's face and handed a big hammer to Eyelashes. 'Now hit the nose bump.'

The soft clunk was barely audible, but when Stonemason Dad pulled the shammy away, the nose clattered to the ground. Part of the herm's mouth had broken, too, and it gave him a lopsided smile.

The god didn't look upset at all. He looked amused.

'Spread out, men!' commanded Alcibiades in a low voice that made his lisp more pronounced. 'Go in groups of two or three. Work quickly and quietly and then meet back here!'

All the men wanted to go with Alcibiades but he said, 'I'll take Euphiletus and the two boys. Your sister had better wait here,' he said to Dinu.

I felt a bit bad for Crina but mainly happy for myself. Alcibiades wanted me on his team!

Dinu had pulled his garland down a little so that it cast his face in shadow.

I didn't have a garland so I started to wrap my scarf around my head.

Not like a girl though.

Like a ninja.

Suddenly Crina grabbed our wrists. 'Alex! Dinu! You can't do this!'

Dinu shook her off.

I tried to be gentler. 'Yes, we can. In fact, we'll be going against history if we don't. Wait here, like Alcibiades said. We'll be back before midnight.'

'You and Dinu could get caught again!' She tugged at my headscarf. 'They could execute you!'

'Not if I'm with Alcibiades!' I rewrapped the scarf around my face.

I had to run in order to catch up.

Alcibiades, Eyelashes and Dinu had stopped by another herm. Eyelashes held the soft leather over the marble face and Alcibiades swung the hammer.

*Thunk!* This time the herm lost its chin as well as its nose.

'Why do boys always want to smash things?' Crina had not done as she was told; she was still following us. 'You're like toddlers knocking down bricks.'

'Smashing things feels good,' I said. 'It makes you feel powerful. And it's better than killing real people.'

Alcibiades cocked his head. 'You try one, Dinu,' he lisped.

Dinu's eyes gleamed with pleasure and I felt a pang of jealousy until Alcibiades looked at me and said, 'Alexis! You help him!'

I held the shammy and Dinu raised the mallet.

His blow took the face right off.

We all grinned. Then Dinu handed me the mallet. 'You next, Alexis,' he said.

Alcibiades gave him a nod of approval.

The mallet was heavy. I felt its power.

'Where's the next one?' I asked.

'I think there's one just up ahead,' said Eyelashes. The strong moonlight on his garland cast leafy shadows on his face.

He turned down a narrow street of white-plastered houses with only a narrow footpath between piled-up dung and rubbish on either side. Thankfully the scarf around my head partly covered my nose and its faint perfume blocked out the worst of the stink.

At the end of this street we turned a corner.

I saw the back of a herm up ahead at a narrow crossroads.

My heart was thudding with excitement and I ran towards it, letting the mallet swing.

But when we reached the moonlit herm, I skidded to a stop and stared.

This one didn't look like Hermes, the messenger god.

It was more like the wise father of satyrs: old Silenus with his bald head, bug eyes, snub nose and wide mouth.

The herm looked just like Socrates.

And that was when I finally came to my senses.

# 47
# Smashing Socrates

'Oh my God!' I felt as if someone had emptied a bucket of ice water on my head. 'What are we doing?'

'What are you waiting for?' cried Dinu. 'Smash it!'

'Yes!' cried Eyelashes. 'Bash it!'

'Come on, Alexis!' lisped Alcibiades. 'Are you with me or against me?'

I let the mallet fall to the street. 'I can't. What would Socrates say?'

'Yes!' hissed Crina. I turned to see her in the shadows, fist-punching the air.

'Socrates doesn't care about the gods of the city!' said Alcibiades. 'He says no true gods would behave as badly as the ones the poets sing of. He believes there must be a single god who is perfectly good and just.'

'That's why he wouldn't do this,' I said. 'It's wrong and you know it.' Then on impulse I added, 'Don't let the black horse drive the chariot of your soul!'

'You dare rebuke me?' A single stride brought Alcibiades so close to me that I could smell the sweet wine on his breath and the musky scent of his sweat. I felt dizzy.

Alcibiades gripped my shoulders. 'Who are you? Who are you really?'

If Socrates' gaze had been like a fishing line, gently trying to tease up the truth from the depths of my mind, Alcibiades' gaze was like a spear piercing my soul.

'What do you mean?' I stammered.

'Nobody has ever seen you before.' He was using the plural form. 'You three just suddenly appeared in the Temple of the Maiden.'

He took my hand and rubbed the palm hard with his calloused thumb.

I yelped.

'Look at this soft hand,' he sneered. 'You've never worked a day in your lives.'

He cocked his head and brought his face so close that his nose was almost touching mine.

'At first I thought you were spies from Corinth. But your Greek is strange and the girl can barely speak it. Therefore not from Corinth. So once again I ask: who are you really?'

My mind was like a hamster on a wheel, working furiously but getting nowhere.

'We're from a faraway land,' I stammered. 'The um . . . Tin Islands.'

'And yet,' he lisped, 'no ship has arrived from such a place and nobody saw you travelling on the road.' He nudged my sandalled foot with the toe of his soft boot. 'Those are the feet of someone who is used to being carried in a litter. Of someone completely unused to walking. But there's something more. It's as if you are not of this world. You don't move like us. You don't even think like us. I think I know who you are, but . . .'

He stood upright and shoved my chest so that I staggered back and almost fell.

'Go on then, leave! Take the girl with you!' He slung an arm around Dinu. 'You won't leave me, will you?'

My best mate turned to Alcibiades. 'No,' he said in Greek. 'I will not leave. I'll stay with you until I die.'

Dinu looked at me and Crina with shadowed eyes. 'I can be a warrior here,' he said in English. 'I will get fame and fortune and *kleos* with Alcibiades. I will never have a life back home as awesome as I can have here.'

Then he picked up the mallet I had discarded and smashed the face of Socrates.

# 48
# Socrates at Home

'Alex?' said Crina half an hour later. 'Do those pillars look pink to you?'

We had risked our lives by walking through the night-time streets of Athens and out the southern gate in a desperate attempt to find the house of Socrates.

We both agreed he was the only one who could talk sense into Alcibiades and Dinu.

Crina had been distracted earlier in the day when the blacksmith's wife had taken her to his house, so she didn't remember the exact route. But she kept recognising landmarks, including the corpse of a dead man in an alley, now partially eaten by dogs.

'I guess those pillars could be pink,' I said. 'It's hard to tell. The moonlight kind of sucks away all the colour.'

'Oh, thank God!' breathed Crina. 'It *is* his house. I recognise the little herm.'

'Do you really think Socrates will answer?' I glanced around the moonlit white houses on the silent street. 'It's the middle of the night!'

'In one of Plato's dialogues, a friend of Socrates came before dawn and woke him up and he didn't even mind.'

'I hope you're right. And I hope he can help,' I said. Then I added, 'I can't believe Dinu wants to stay.'

'I can. I love my brother but he's a good-looking bully, just like Alcibiades. But he's nowhere near as clever. He hasn't thought this through.'

We had reached the house with the faded pillars. The stone herm was only as tall as me, crudely carved and with a gentle smile.

'Please may Socrates help us!' I put my right hand under the herm's bearded chin in the way I'd seen others do.

'I think he carved that one himself,' said Crina, and also touched the underside of his chin. Then she stepped into the porch, made her hand into a fist and banged on the door.

Nothing.

She banged again.

Somewhere nearby, a dog began to bark.

Then another took up the refrain.

And another.

A line of a poem suddenly came to me, something my gran always recites when we hear barking dogs:

*In the nightmare of the dark, all the dogs of Athens bark.*

Crina muttered a prayer and banged a third time. 'O Socrates!' she called out. 'You speak the truth!'

Now it seemed that all the dogs in Athens were barking. But there was another sound. From behind the faded blue door came the wail of a crying baby, then a woman's shrill voice and finally the gentle muttering of a man.

Presently the door opened and Socrates peered out at us. He was wearing his grubby himation, but instead of a walking stick he held a naked baby boy in his arms.

'By the dog!' he exclaimed mildly. 'What are you two doing here at this time of night?'

But before we could answer he turned and called over his shoulder. 'Xanthippe! Prepare some warm wine!'

He beckoned us inside and led us to a little table with two stools near a shaggy pistachio tree. I spotted a ceramic baby potty just like one in the British Museum. Socrates pulled it over and cheerfully used it as a third stool for himself.

I knew we didn't have much time, but our feet were aching and our stomachs were growling, so we sat gratefully. The moon was so bright that we didn't even need a lamp.

Socrates' yawning wife brought three cups, plus half a loaf of brown bread and a little saucer of olives. She was very pregnant and her hair was tied up in a scarf.

'Alexis, this is my long-suffering wife, Xanthippe. Crina met her this morning.'

Xanthippe snorted and disappeared into the kitchen. A few moments later she was back with a bronze jug from which she poured steaming liquid. Its smell reminded me of the mulled wine they serve at St Nektarios church after the Christmas morning service.

Xanthippe settled herself in a wicker chair a few paces from us and began to make yarn with a drop spindle.

Still holding his baby son, Socrates let a few drops spatter from his cup to the ground and murmured a prayer. Then he drank. Crina and I followed his example.

The wine was sweet and hot and spicy. Together with the bread and olives, it sparked a flame of hope. While we ate, I quickly told Socrates how Alcibiades and his friends were smashing the herms.

Even by moonlight, I could see his face go a shade paler.

'This will not end well,' he said.

'Goo!' said the baby. One of his chubby hands caught Socrates' beard and held it fast.

'Dear little Lamprocles,' he murmured. 'What a world we have brought you into! I wonder where your soul resided before now.'

Then I told him how Dinu wanted to stay with Alcibiades.

'Alcibiades has that effect on people, doesn't he?' Socrates gazed down at his baby son, who gurgled happily.

'Dinu has to come home with us tonight,' I said. 'We need to be at the Temple of the Maiden by midnight.'

Socrates gave me a keen look. 'Interesting that your way home is by the temple,' he said.

Before I could think of some explanation he turned to Crina. 'And if your brother is not with you?' he said, speaking slowly and clearly.

'It will hurt mother heart,' said Crina in her broken Greek. 'Very bad. Very, very bad.'

'It will be as if he died,' I said simply.

'How can I help?'

'Can you convince Alcibiades to tell Dinu to go home with us?'

'I doubt it. He stopped listening to me long ago. You'd do better trying to convince your friend.'

'Please?'

For a long moment, Socrates looked down at the baby in his arms. Then he got to his feet. 'Xanthippe, my dear, I must escort these children back to town.'

She put down her wool and spindle, stood up and handed him his walking stick in exchange for the baby. Later I read many stories of what a bad wife Xanthippe was, always nagging him and once even throwing the contents of a chamber pot at his head, but I will always remember her with gratitude.

Before we left she gave us a tired smile and a prayer. 'May your beloved Apollo bring you safely home tonight, dear husband.' Then she looked at me and Crina. 'And may

Hermes the messenger god see you and your brother safely back to your native land.'

As we stepped out of the courtyard back into night-time Athens, I was glad of those prayers. In the next hour, we would need all the help we could get.

# 49

# Little Divine Voice

When my mum was alive she never used to let me go on a sleepover if the moon was full. She said the full moon made people crazy and that more crimes occurred on those nights. My dad said there were no statistics to support her theory, but she stuck by her beliefs.

It certainly seemed like my mum was right that particular summer night in the year 415 BC.

The first thing we came across on our way back into town with Socrates was two men digging a hole in the wall of a house. Socrates ran at them, yelling some kind of battle cry and waving his walking stick. The men ran away, but his shout set off some of the dogs in the area.

'Who were they?' I asked him when he came back. 'What were they doing?'

Socrates' bushy eyebrows went up in surprise. 'Wall-diggers. Thieves.'

I said to Crina, 'I think the ancient Greek word for "burglar" is "wall-digger".'

The barking dogs had set off others, and soon it seemed that every dog in Athens was joining in.

'Thank goodness they're in their owners' houses,' I whispered to Crina. 'They say the famous Athenian playwright Euripides died by being torn into pieces by a watchdog.'

She shuddered, then screamed as a massive dog emerged from the inky shadows of an alley.

Unlike all the other dogs, this one was not barking. It was growling.

'Get behind me and don't move,' said Socrates. 'I know this beast. He killed a child last month.'

I grabbed Crina's hand and pulled her behind Socrates with me. 'He said don't move,' I hissed.

She nodded and froze. I could feel her trembling.

For the second time that day Socrates shielded us from danger.

He spoke gently to the hound, but the animal must have smelled Crina's fear and maybe mine too. He snarled and sprang at us.

Almost casually Socrates swung his stick, giving the hound a sharp crack on the head. The dog staggered to one side and then came at us again, but less enthusiastically. This time Socrates crouched and jabbed the stick forward, like a spear.

It hit the big dog squarely on the chest.

Once again the creature staggered. But this time he didn't come at us; he hesitated.

Socrates gave him a third sharp crack on the head and the dog ran whimpering into the shadows.

Crina and I stared at each other in amazement.

'Ninja Socrates!' I whispered.

She nodded, then looked down at her right hand, which was still clasped in my left.

When I let go, she looked disappointed.

No time to process that now.

Socrates was already striding ahead with his famous pelican walk: head swinging right and left, glaring eyes on the lookout for any further attacks, canine or otherwise.

Then we saw what the herm-busters had done to one of the marble guardians of the crossroads.

The first herm we had smashed ended up with an amused expression. But this one looked as if it had been ravaged by some flesh-eating virus. It was horrible.

Socrates shook his head sadly, then resumed walking.

'Alex,' whispered Crina, as we fell into step behind him. 'What will we do if Dinu won't come back with us?'

'I don't know.'

'Mother would blame me,' said Crina. 'She'd never forgive me.'

'We've just got to find him and convince him,' I said. I

wanted to cheer her up so I said, 'I can always use my secret weapon to lure him back to our time.'

She gave me a blank look and I had to explain. 'Salt-and-vinegar crisps.'

'Yeah, but they eat bread dipped in vinegar for breakfast here,' she pointed out. 'Which apparently tastes like soggy salt-and-vinegar crisps.'

'Oh no! You're right,' I groaned.

We were almost at the south side of the Acropolis where one day there would be a giant car park, when we bumped into the back of Socrates.

He had stopped walking and stood stock-still in the centre of the moonlit road, leaning on his staff.

At first I thought another dog must be attacking us. I grabbed Crina and pulled her close to me.

But there was no dog.

Socrates was staring at the ground.

I looked down too, but couldn't see anything down there except a scattering of olive-shaped droppings where a flock of goats must have passed by earlier.

I remembered Glaucon telling me how when they were on campaign, Socrates once stood in a trance for nearly a whole day without moving.

I let go of Crina's hand and went around to see Socrates' face. 'Are you all right, sir?' I asked.

'I'm sorry,' he said, looking up from under his eyebrows.

'I can't go any further with you.'

'But we need you to talk to Alcibiades. To convince him to let Dinu come home with us.'

'I can't. My *daimonion* just stopped me.'

'Your *daimonion*?' I echoed. 'Your little demon?'

'It's a divine sign I've had since I was a child. A kind of inner voice that stops me from doing something or going somewhere. Like in the Agora, when the chariot was driving at us. And just now when the dog approached.'

'Shall we wait, too?'

'No, you must go on. Find your friend. Try to convince him to go with you.'

'What's wrong?' Crina asked me. 'Why have we stopped?'

'He can't go any further because he's hearing voices.'

'Oh no!'

Socrates was still staring at the ground. Crina grabbed his arm and pulled. 'Come, O Socrates!' she said. 'Come!'

He stood as solidly as a tree rooted to the ground. 'I can't,' he said gently. 'I must obey the god.'

# 50
# Know Thyself

'Alex!' Crina turned to me. 'Do something!'

Standing stock-still in the moonlight, Socrates resembled a herm. That reminded me that the way to ask a god or powerful person for a favour was to touch them under the chin. I hate begging, but time was running out.

I touched Socrates under his beard. It was quite soft and I could feel the pulse beating there. 'Please, Socrates?'

'I'm sorry, but no.'

Then I remembered you could also clasp someone's knees.

I brushed away the goat droppings, knelt down on the hard-packed earth of the road and wrapped my arms around his knobbly knees. His legs were as solid as oak.

'Please?'

'*Ooda moce*,' he said softly. No way.

'Come on, Alex!' Crina was close to tears. 'He doesn't care about us.'

I looked up at him. 'Didn't you say that the only thing people should consider is whether they are acting rightly or wrongly?'

'Yes!' Socrates let his walking stick drop so he could unwrap my arms and pull me gently to my feet. 'Because it is your eternal soul that is important, not your perishable body.'

'Then why won't you help us?'

'Because I know myself.' He bent to pick up his walking stick.

I cursed and turned away.

Crina looked at me. 'He won't come, will he?'

'No.'

'He said he knows himself, didn't he?'

I nodded.

A tear ran down her face and she angrily rubbed it away.

Socrates patted her head with his free hand and then gripped my shoulder the way my dad used to do.

'Go!' His keen eyes gleamed in the moonlight. 'Find your friend. My little divine voice sometimes urges me to hold back my companions too, but it is not preventing you. And I believe your words will be more convincing than mine. Farewell.'

I swallowed an angry reply and turned away. 'Come on, Crina! We can't go home without Dinu, and I don't want to spend another minute in this horrible place.'

We left Socrates standing like a herm in the moonlit road. The dogs had stopped barking and only the throb of the cicadas could be heard.

The half-hour that followed was the darkest I have ever known.

My legs ached from walking miles. My sandals were giving me blisters. My stomach churned with the mulled wine. And I was pretty sure I had picked up lice from somewhere. I felt them crawling in my hair.

Then I stepped in a puddle of something disgusting and slimy. I didn't even want to know what it was.

Crina and I moved towards the Acropolis as quietly as we could, not wanting to disturb another ancient Rottweiler. Coming around a corner we found ourselves facing the creepiest broken herm so far. A blow of the hammer had transformed his smiling mouth into a hole that seemed permanently open in a silent scream.

'I don't like this reality,' whimpered Crina. 'I want to go home.'

'I know.' My scalp was crawling. Or rather, something was crawling on my scalp. I caught it and held it out in the moonlight between the fingernails of my forefinger and thumb. A louse. I shuddered and flicked it away. 'I want to go home, too.'

'Alex?'

'Yes?'

'You know we can't go home without Dinu, don't you? If we leave him here, it will be as if he died.'

'But if we stay here too, it will be as if *we* died. And if we go back without him your mother will blame us.'

'She'll blame me,' said Crina. 'I know it. Nothing Dinu or Mari does is ever wrong. I'm the only one who messes up.'

'If you don't go back, then neither will I.'

'Really?'

'Really.' I felt for her hand and gripped it tightly.

She stopped and turned to face me in the moonlight. 'You'd stay for me?'

I nodded.

Above the soft creaking of the cicadas I heard Athena's owl hoot, as if to say, 'Wise decision.'

'We'll have to live a quiet life,' I said. 'Maybe on a farm somewhere out in the country. Our main job will be to avoid changing the future, or all the people we love will go *kerpluff*.'

'But you took this job to become rich and famous. Living on a little farm in the countryside would be the opposite of that.'

'Alcibiades is the richest, most famous man of this time. And look what it's done to him.'

The hoot of the owl came again from somewhere up ahead. This time it sounded wrong.

'Did you hear that?' I said.

'The wood pigeon?'

'I thought it was an owl.'

'It's not a wood pigeon or an owl, you idiots,' said a familiar voice from the shadows a little way up the road. 'It's me.'

# 51

# Not an Owl

'**D**inu?' Crina and I said his name at the same time.

A figure emerged from the blackness beneath a fig tree. It was Dinu, still wearing his banquet garland.

'Thank God!' Crina ran to him and threw her arms around him. He hugged her back, and after a while he raised his face to look at me. 'Dude! It's good to see you.'

I came forward to give him a fist bump but he was wiping his face with his forearm.

My stomach flipped.

'Dinu,' I said. 'Have you been crying?'

'No,' he said.

Strong moonlight on the garland threw his face in shadow, but when I pushed the leaves away I saw his swollen eyes and wet cheeks.

'You *have* been crying!' I said. 'Did something happen to Alcibiades? Did they catch him?'

Then Crina gasped. 'Dinu! You're hurt!' She caught his wrist and lifted his right hand. Moonlight showed a bloody linen strip around the tip of the middle finger.

The sight of it made my toes curl.

'Dude. What happened?'

'Alcibiades told me to touch his sword. To test the sharpness of its edge.'

'And?'

'I lost the tip of my finger.'

Crina gasped again.

Dinu hung his head. 'Alcibiades laughed . . . he *laughed*! Then he asked me if I'd even seen a sword before.'

'Did you tell him you're the best at *Ancient Greek Assassins*?'

'That's just a stupid game. The sword I touched was real. I never thought anything could be that sharp . . . When they finished bandaging it he asked me to bring him his shield. I could barely lift it. They laughed even more, and one of them said, "Is this your new right-hand man?" and he said, "I don't think so, especially not now." And he laughed again.'

'But he promised to train you. I was there. I heard him say it.'

Dinu snorted. 'He's like every other politician in the world: a big fat liar.'

'Then what happened?' Crina asked.

'Then they left me. They all went off together, laughing and singing.'

'Oh, Dinu.' She reached out to comfort him, but he pushed her hand away.

'So will you come back with us now?' I said.

'God, yes!'

'And I don't have to go through some Socratic Q and A to convince you to come?'

'God, no!' He took off his garland and threw it on the ground.

Without the garland he looked like Dinu again.

'Come on then, big bro,' said Crina. 'Let's go home.'

'There's a problem,' he said, and pulled us back into the inky shadows of the fig tree.

'What?' Crina and I said together.

'The entrance to the Acropolis is crawling with guards – Scythian archers and citizens with swords.'

'But it must be nearly midnight,' I hissed. 'The portal will be turned on at any minute.'

Crina said, 'What about the path we used in the twenty-first century, on the south side of the Acropolis, via the Theatre of Dionysus?'

'There are men there too.'

Suddenly Crina gripped my arm. 'I might know a way! Simona told me there were steep stairs on the other side.'

'When?'

'When you were sleeping. She showed me her loom upstairs and some of the cloth she had woven. When she was younger she lived up there for nearly a year to help weave a giant cloak for the statue of the goddess. She said that she and the other girls sometimes went out onto narrow stairs so she could see her house.'

'Narrow stairs?' I said. 'Are you sure?'

Crina nodded. 'Simona mimed it for me. She pointed through her window at the Acropolis and made her fingers walk up imaginary stairs.'

'If she could see her house then those stairs must be on the north slope,' I said.

'She's right!' Dinu cried suddenly. 'In *Ancient Greek Assassins* there are some stairs on the north face.' Then his shoulders slumped. 'But once you get to the top you need to use your sticky-monkey abilities.'

'Wait,' I mused. 'If there are stairs there must be a door.'

'I'm telling you, it's there!' said Crina.

I nodded. 'Let's look. It's our only chance.'

'Come on then,' said Dinu. 'I think I know the way.' He led us out of the shade of the fig tree and past some houses.

The sole of my sandal was coming unstuck and it made a slapping sound as we ran.

We were going up an alley between two houses, one with freshly plastered outer walls and the other crumbling, when we all heard the growl of a dog.

We froze. Crina pointed at my sandal and raised her eyebrows.

She was right. One barking dog could betray our position to guards.

I took off the offending sandal and left it at the side of the road. We managed to creep on past the house without setting off the canine burglar alarm again.

Up ahead, Dinu was crouching behind some shrubs with his finger to his lips in the universal gesture for silence.

When Crina and I reached him, we both recoiled at the smell. People obviously used these bushes as a toilet.

Dinu pointed at the dark shape of the Acropolis rearing up above us. Then he made his fingers act out walking up stairs.

Although this side of the mini-mountain was in shadow, we could glimpse pale stairs winding up between boulders and scrubby bushes.

'That must be the way up,' he mouthed. 'But there are two guards on either side of that path.'

I whispered, 'We need to get them to move away.'

Crina said, 'I have an idea. Take off your other sandal.'

'Why?'

'To toss into the courtyard with the dog. His barking will make them go there to investigate.'

'Good idea!' I slipped off my other sandal.

I had one chance.

I took a deep breath, pulled back my arm and let go.

We all watched the shoe arc up into the sky and then

drop down smack bang into the courtyard. A moment's silence and then the night was shattered by outraged barking.

'Well done, Alex!' said Crina, and Dinu added, 'Nice one!'

As both guards moved away, towards the sound of the barking dog, the three of us ran forward in a crouch. We kept to the shadows as much as we could and tried to avoid those bushes that had been used as toilets.

Stone steps carved into the face of the hill led us up between boulders and thorny bushes. I could smell thyme and sage, the scent of Greece.

Down below, the dogs had stopped barking. In the bushes around us cicadas were chirping urgently, as if to say, '*Go, go, go!*'

The steps grew narrower as we ascended.

Once Crina slipped and nearly fell.

I was following behind and managed to catch her, but for a moment I thought we might both go over.

'Soles too slippery.' She kicked off her sandals and carried on barefoot like me.

Dinu was ahead of us and I started to notice dark drops on the stone steps. His finger was bleeding again.

'*Go, go, go!*' urged the cicadas.

By the time we finally reached the top of the stairs, my legs were on fire and my heart was almost pounding out of my chest. A vertical wall of massive stone blocks was set with a wooden door. The door was small, but it was made of oak and it was thick.

Dinu took a deep breath, pushed and then cursed in Romanian.

He turned, still panting from the climb, and gave us a bleak look.

'Locked!' he said simply. 'The door is locked.'

# 52
# The Key

Sometimes late at night when I can't sleep, I think about that moment at the top of the stairs and shudder.

We were so close to the portal.

And yet so far.

Our time was almost up.

The prospect of even another twenty-four hours in ancient Athens was like a death sentence.

Dejectedly I sat on the threshold of the locked door and put my head in my hands. Crina sat down on one side of me then Dinu slumped down on the other. The stone slab was just wide enough for the three of us. On Dinu's right was a steep drop down and on Crina's left was a sheer vertical wall up.

'What are we going to do?' whispered Crina.

'I don't know.' I put my arm around her and gave her shoulders an encouraging squeeze. But I had never felt worse.

'Guys, I'm sorry.' Dinu leaned back against the door. 'This was all my fault for wanting to be rich and famous. And thinking it would be cool to kill Spartans for real.'

'No, it wasn't,' I said. 'I was the one who got tempted by fame and fortune.'

'If it was anybody's fault it was mine,' said Crina, 'for crashing through the portal and getting you arrested.'

'No point playing the blame game,' I said.

Dinu put his head between his knees and panted. 'I don't feel too good.'

I glanced at him. The brilliant moonlight showed blood still dripping from his finger.

Moonlight?

I looked up. 'Oh no!'

'What?'

'The moon!'

'What about it?'

'A few minutes ago we were safe in the shadows. Now it's lighting us up like a spotlight. Any moment one of the archers will look up and see us . . .'

Crina gripped my arm. 'Come on, Alex! Think of something!'

'Yeah, Wimpy!' Dinu tried to grin. 'Don't fail us now.'

My heart sank.

They were both looking to me for a solution.

I had nothing.

There was only one place to turn.

Sometimes when I pray to God, an image pops into my head. It comes really fast, sometimes as I'm forming the prayer.

Even as I murmured the words 'O Lord, please help,' the image of a doormat popped into my head.

'Doormat?' I muttered.

'What?'

I shook my head. 'Does the word "doormat" mean anything to you?'

'We keep our spare key under our doormat,' said Dinu. 'In case one of us gets home and Mother isn't in.'

Crina turned away.

Maybe she was hiding tears of despair.

Then she turned back.

'Alex, is this what an ancient Greek key looks like?'

She was holding something like a little iron rake turned back on itself.

'Oh my God, yes!' My jaw dropped. 'Where on earth did you get that?'

'In a hole under a rock, right here by the wall.' She pointed with her chin.

Dinu forced a weak grin. 'The ancient version of a doormat,' he said.

I nodded. 'I guess human nature doesn't change.' A surge of renewed energy brought me to my feet.

'Let's just pray it works!' Crina said.

In modern times keys are little flat things you can fit in your wallet. This one was the size of my fist.

I stuck it in and tried to twist it.

Nothing.

Even modern keys sometimes need a certain touch.

I took a deep breath. Told myself to stay calm. And tried again. Still nothing.

Then I remembered that ancient keys don't release a hidden tumbler; they lift a crossbeam. I had been twisting when I should have been lifting.

I lifted the key and felt the mechanism work and heard the creak of the crossbeam.

'Push!' I commanded between gritted teeth.

Dinu and Crina both pushed.

And the door swung open.

We fell through with gasps of relief.

Then Dinu said, 'Hurry or we'll miss the portal. Please.'

We sprinted through a herb garden with a statue of a female goddess at its centre and out through a gate onto the Acropolis.

The Parthenon was straight ahead.

And the moon was high above.

We were in the right place at the right time.

We might just make it.

'Come on!' I said.

'Which end is the portal?' asked Crina.

'That end!' I pointed. 'The east.'

I led the way, pulling Crina by the hand as we wove through the moonlit forest of bronze and marble statues. We had almost reached the far end of the Parthenon when we heard a noise that chilled us.

'Xtop!' said a voice in a Scythian accent. 'Xtop or I'll shoot!'

We stopped and slowly turned to see a figure emerge from behind a big altar. It was one of the Scythian archers.

I had not seen this one before. He was short and stocky with a white beard.

He looked more like a Smurf than any of the others.

In fact, apart from not being blue, he looked just like Papa Smurf.

I couldn't help it: I burst out laughing.

That was when he shot Dinu.

# 53
# Last Words

That moment might have been less awful if Dinu had screamed. Instead he just stared in horror at the arrow sticking out of his upper arm.

The old Scythian had already notched another and was aiming it.

I started to grab Crina and Dinu to pull them down but I was too late.

The archer had already let fly.

But for some reason the arrow went soaring up into the air as the Scythian slumped slowly to the ground.

And now a snub-nosed, balding, bearded guy was bending over Papa Smurf, prodding him with a walking stick.

'Socrates!' gasped Crina. 'Help!'

Socrates lifted his head then hurried towards us.

'Dinu's been shot!' I cried.

'I can see.' Socrates went round behind Dinu. 'Thank

whatever gods you believe in,' he said. 'The point has gone right through. It will be easy to pull out.'

'Did you kill the archer?' Dinu's voice was faint.

'No. That one has a thick skull. He'll come round soon.'

I turned to Socrates. 'Thank you for saving us. But what about your little divine voice?'

Without looking up from examining the arrow he said, 'As soon as my *daimonion* stopped preventing me, I came. Those stairs are steep! Now, am I right in thinking you need to go into the temple?'

'Yes,' I said. 'We need to go into the Parthenon now, so, um . . . the goddess will take us home. But we can't go with the arrow in him,' I added.

I didn't add that the bronze or iron arrowhead was inorganic and might explode in the portal, taking off his whole arm.

'Then I must pull out the arrow and bind the wound.'

I looked at Dinu. 'You ready for this?'

My friend's face was dead white. He swallowed hard. And nodded.

Socrates went behind Dinu.

'Clench your teeth. I will pull it out as quickly as I can,' said Socrates. 'You two, hold him.'

I gave Dinu a strong bear hug, clamping his elbows to his torso. Crina gripped his lower arms.

Socrates grabbed the arrow and pulled.

Dinu screamed.

Then he fainted.

I would have fainted, too, but I was concentrating on holding my friend so he wouldn't bang his head.

Crina and I eased Dinu down onto the cold marble. Then we watched as Socrates expertly tore a strip from the hem of Dinu's gauzy chiton and bound it around the bleeding hole in Dinu's arm.

'What are you doing?' mumbled Dinu in English as Socrates finished tying off the makeshift bandage.

'Socrates saved us,' I said. 'Then he pulled out the arrow and he's just binding up your wound.'

'Thank you,' Dinu managed to say in Greek. He was literally as white as marble.

'Dinu,' said Crina in English, 'we have to get out of here. Now.'

I looked at Socrates. 'May we go?'

The philosopher nodded. 'My *daimonion* does not forbid you. Go with the gods and remember: the unexamined life is not worth living. Don't let a single day pass without discussing what is good for your soul.'

'*Alay-thay leg-ace, O Soak-rah-tace,*' said Crina solemnly. You speak the truth, O Socrates.

Then she gave him a quick hug.

'Farewell, O Socrates.' I swallowed hard. 'Thank you for saving us.'

Dinu simply said, 'Thank you, O Socrates.'

Then, with me and Crina supporting Dinu, one on each side, we made for the Parthenon, praying that the doors of the temple would be open and that we would not be too late.

## 54

# Back to the Future

When we came back through the portal to the twenty-first-century Parthenon, Mr Posh was there to meet us. The Athens police had summoned him from London after Solomon Daisy claimed to be working for MI5.

Decorum prevents me telling you what happened to me and Crina and Dinu after we came through the portal. Both Dinu's wounds were bleeding again but because we had disobeyed rule number two – *drink, don't eat* – that wasn't the worst of it. Needless to say, there was a lot of mess to clean up.

The three of us have taken a solemn vow never to speak of it again.

Mr Posh told Gran and Dinu's mum that a terrorist had shot Dinu in the arm with a crossbow at the very moment the three of us had gone outside for some fresh air. And that some torture had been involved. That would explain Dinu's arrow wound and the missing tip of his finger.

He explained that the Greek government had hushed it up so as not to credit the group claiming to have done it.

He said that a large amount of money would be paid to both our families as compensation.

The three of us, he said, were being kept in police custody for our own safety.

In actual fact we spent several hours in various showers and decontamination rooms.

All of us had to be debugged.

Literally.

In only twenty-four hours we had all picked up ticks, lice and fleas. The unholy trinity.

After they'd cleaned us up and tended to Dinu's wounds and given us fresh clothes – oh, the joy of jeans and trainers! – Mr Posh took us to a debriefing at the British School in Athens.

Our debriefing room was an old-fashioned library with wooden shelves divided by pilasters painted the deep red of an Athenian pot. It had a wooden floor, high windows and a lofty white ceiling and door.

Eight of us sat on straight-backed chairs around one of the long wooden tables: me, Dinu, Crina, Mr Posh and Solomon Daisy. There was a woman from MI5 who doubled as a security guard and a child protector. I'm not even allowed to make up a name for her. And there were two experts on

Socrates: a pretty Greek lady archaeologist called Dr Fotini Charis and an Oxford professor called Armand D'Angour.

Athens-born Dr Charis had done her PhD at Cambridge and now taught philosophy at the University of Athens. Professor D'Angour had written a book called *Socrates in Love* and happened to be in Athens for a conference.

'See the books on that wall behind you?' Dr Charis pointed with a pearly-tipped forefinger. 'They are all by Plato or about Socrates or both.'

My jaw dropped. 'There must be over a thousand.'

'Over two thousand, though not all are on display. And keep in mind, this is a small institution specialising in archaeology.'

Professor D'Angour leaned forward. 'Every university of any repute offers courses on Platonic philosophy. And for over two thousand years scholars have devoted their lives to studying Socrates and Plato.'

'Like me,' said Dr Charis. 'I've been obsessed with him since my father took me to the Agora museum when I was eight.'

'I was taught ancient Greek at school from when I was ten,' said Professor D'Angour. 'And I fell in love with the language immediately.'

'You will have quite some job convincing us you really went back in time.' Dr Charis raised both eyebrows, which were very black and straight.

So we told them everything we could think of.

About ten minutes in they were both smiling and nodding and taking lots of notes.

After about two hours we had exhausted the subject of Socrates, Alcibiades and Kid Plato. Professor D'Angour was disappointed that we hadn't met Aspasia, the quick-witted widow of Pericles whom Socrates had known in earlier days and might even have fallen in love with. But he was delighted to hear about how ancient Greek music sounded, since that was his particular field of research. Dr Charis made us describe the clothing they wore and the artefacts they used.

Finally, after three hours of intensive questioning we convinced them that we really had gone back.

Someone brought in Greek coffee and Orangina, along with a big platter of baklava.

As he sipped his coffee, Professor D'Angour told us that although Socrates was considered ugly when he was older, he was probably not bad-looking as a younger man, when he was admired for his physique and courage on the battlefield.

'*Jolie-laid*,' he said. 'It's French for "ugly in a pretty way". If they make a movie of my book, I'd like Adrian Grenier to play the part.'

'Why not a Greek actor?' asked Dr Charis, sucking baklava honey from her long-nailed fingers. 'Omiros Poulakis has a snub nose, and the way he looks up at you from under his eyebrows would be perfect.'

Crina put down her Orangina. 'Rami Malek,' she said. 'He'd make a good Socrates.'

'Somehow I can't imagine Socrates singing "Bohemian Rhapsody" by Queen,' I quipped. That got everyone laughing.

Solomon Daisy had been quiet all this time, but suddenly his head was in his hands and his massive shoulders were shaking.

We all stopped laughing and stared at him.

Was he laughing or crying?

'Mr Daisy?' asked Mr Posh.

He raised his face. It was wet and smiling.

'That's all I wanted to know,' he said, looking at me and Dinu and Crina in turn. 'That's why I sent you back. To see if Socrates was really true. True in the deepest sense. You have satisfied my dearest wish.' To Mr Posh he said, 'I'll make myself completely transparent and show you all my offshore accounts. You can lock me away if you like. I've learned my lesson.'

Mr Posh raised a sceptical eyebrow. 'Very touching. But I think there are better places for you than prison. The Prime Minister would like to see you and your two technicians as soon as we return to the UK,' he said. 'I think we can come to a mutually agreeable arrangement.'

# 55
# Soul Butterflies

Later that afternoon as the day started to cool, Professor D'Angour and Dr Charis took Mr Posh and us three kids around the Agora, which is now just a bunch of ruins with trees and tortoises and butterflies.

Crina whispered to me and Dinu, 'Does Dr Charis remind you of anybody?'

'The shoemaker's daughter,' said Dinu and I nodded.

'Doctor Charis,' I began.

'Please call me Fotini.'

'Are you from Athens?'

'Yes, as far back as records go,' she replied, 'on my mother's side. Why?'

'You remind us of Simona, the daughter of Simon the Shoemaker,' said Crina boldly.

Dr Charis stopped in her tracks, removed her sunglasses and turned to look at us. 'When I was young I had to wear an eyepatch to correct a lazy eye. And my great-great-grandfather claimed to have come from a long line of shoemakers.'

We all stared at her and Mr Posh murmured, 'Extraordinary.'

After a moment we continued on through the knee-high grasses and wildflowers of the ruined Agora.

Presently Professor D'Angour stopped at the remains of a building near the Tholos. 'Any idea what this is?' he said. He held up his hand to stop me speaking. 'Not you, Alex. You've been to Athens several times. I want to know if Dinu or Crina can tell me.'

Crina got it first. 'It's the house of Simon the Shoemaker!'

'Brava!' He stepped to one side and we all saw a stone block on the waist-high foundations behind him. It bore the inscription 'OIKIA SIMONOS - HOUSE OF SIMON' picked out in red paint.

'And look!' Dr Charis used the toe of her sandal to tap another stone half-hidden in the golden grass. It read 'I AM THE BOUNDARY OF THE AGORA' in both Greek and English.

I shivered.

And as we started up a path towards the Acropolis, I shivered again. I knew where we were heading.

About a hundred paces on, we stopped by some ruins lying beside the trench of the Great Drain. It was very quiet here, with the late sun shining through the trees. A few birds twittered and a bee buzzed past my right ear.

'See the foundations of this building?' said Professor D'Angour. 'It's the State Prison where Alex and Dinu almost ended up. It's probably also the place where Socrates spent the last month of his life before he bravely faced execution.'

Mr Posh frowned. 'I thought the Prison of Socrates was some caves near the Acropolis.'

'Almost certainly not,' said Dr Charis. 'Archaeologists found little cups for measuring hemlock here and even a votive figurine of Socrates himself, as if it became a kind of shrine to his memory.'

'He died with extreme calm and dignity, didn't he?' asked Mr Posh.

'Yes,' replied Professor D'Angour. 'While his friends wept, he calmly drank the deadly potion. It makes you numb and cold from the feet up,' he added.

Dr Charis said, 'We know this because Plato wrote a blow-by-blow account of Socrates' last hours in a dialogue called *Phaedo.*'

'Even though he tells us that he wasn't actually present when Socrates died,' added the professor.

'But Plato *was* present at the trial of Socrates, and wrote about it in an account called *The Apology.*'

'Which really means a defence, rather than an apology,' added Crina.

'Exactly.' Dr Charis took off her sunglasses and looked at

us. 'It's one of the few dialogues that's not a dialogue, that is to say a question-and-answer session. Plato only reports what Socrates says, and for once Socrates plainly states his beliefs.'

'What was the charge?' I asked.

'They accused him of corrupting the youth and introducing new gods,' said Dr Charis. 'And I do believe he was guilty.'

We all stared at her.

She put on her sunglasses again. 'Not of corrupting the youth,' she said. 'But Socrates believed an extraordinary thing: he believed that *ho theos* – that is, God or "the god" – must be purely good and must want people to try to be good too. To be virtuous. To seek *aretay*.'

'*Aretay* means "virtue" or "excellence",' I whispered to Crina.

Mr Posh raised an eyebrow. 'Are you claiming Socrates didn't believe in the Greek gods?'

'I am. I believe he sacrificed to them and paid them lip service,' said Dr Charis, 'but he thought they were cruel and capricious, which they are. So in a way he *was* introducing new gods. Or rather *a* new god. That is why Socrates is still revered by many Jews and Christians.'

Crina frowned. 'But he lived five hundred years before Christ.'

'Yes, he did.'

'Some historians think the charges were merely an excuse to arrest him,' said the professor. 'The Athenians really wanted to punish the maverick general Alcibiades, but by

266

that time he was already dead. So they executed his teacher instead: Socrates.'

Dinu looked at him. 'Why did the Athenians want to kill Alcibiades?'

'Many reasons,' said Professor D'Angour. 'Mainly because the Sicilian Expedition was a terrible disaster. As you know, it resulted in the deaths of more than twenty thousand Athenian soldiers. As a consequence Athens lost the war with Sparta and ultimately her empire.'

'But I thought Alcibiades never went on the expedition,' I said.

'He didn't. But it was originally his idea. And even before the expedition set out, the Athenians voted for him to be put to death on account of the incident of the herms and the profaning of the Mysteries. So he defected to Sparta—'

'What?' Dinu's face went a shade paler.

'In fairness, the council had voted for him to be put to death.'

'But he fought for the Spartans against Athens?'

'Yes,' agreed the professor. 'Even so, when he changed sides again and returned a few years later the Athenians gave him a hero's welcome.'

Dr Charis added, 'We Athenians have a strange love-hate relationship with Alcibiades.'

'Like in that famous poem by Catullus,' suggested Mr Posh.

'*Odi et amo*,' I quoted the Latin. 'I hate and I love . . .'

'Yes.' Professor D'Angour smiled.

'How did Alcibiades die?' Dinu asked in a barely audible voice.

'Accounts vary,' said the professor. 'But historians agree that he'd fled to Phrygia, that is modern Turkey. He was hiding out in a house with his latest girlfriend, and Persian commandos tracked him down. They had been sent at the request of the Spartan king, who was in league with the local Persian governor. The soldiers set the house on fire to drive Alcibiades out.'

'Oh!' Crina covered her mouth with her hand.

'Then what?' Dinu's face was pale.

'He charged outside, naked except for a blanket wrapped around his left arm as a shield, and they shot him full of arrows. It was only five years later that they put his teacher Socrates to death.'

After hearing that, we were all silent for a while.

It was hot and peaceful there, with golden grasses around the foundations of the cell where Socrates had spent the last month of his life. Twig birds were twittering and a wood pigeon was cooing. We could hear faint music coming from one of the cafes. A couple of girls came by, in shorts and sunglasses, with their bare arms already turning pink. They looked around then turned and headed back, because the path ended there.

I wanted to shout after them, 'This is the spot where one of the most amazing men in the history of the world died!'

Professor D'Angour, Dr Charis, Mr Posh and Dinu started back along the path, but Crina and I lingered at the ruins of the prison.

'Do you think Socrates guessed we were from the future?' she asked me.

'No idea,' I said. 'In a way, I don't think that would have mattered. He only wanted each of us to live our best life.'

'And I intend to,' she said.

I glanced at her and smiled. 'Me too.'

At that moment a little white butterfly fluttered by.

'Goodbye, Socrates,' I whispered.

And Crina added, 'We'll never forget you.'

# 56
# Back to School

When Dinu and I came into the cafeteria on the first day back at school after the summer holidays, the whole place fell silent again. But just for a moment: then chairs scraped and feet pounded as a bunch of kids rushed towards us. I saw a kind of hunger in their eyes, as if they hoped some of our popularity would rub off on them.

It reminded me of the way the crowds had looked when Alcibiades drove past in his chariot. Or when Socrates did his pelican walk through the forum. I now knew those were the same people who had later urged the death penalty for both men. *Hoi polloi.* The masses.

I braced myself for fake smiles and demands for selfies, but to my surprise the masses swarmed right on past.

Dinu and I turned to see them mobbing a red-headed girl named Britney in our year.

'What the chickens?' Dinu muttered, reaching for a tray.

I shrugged as I grabbed one too. 'No idea.'

Crina came up to us. She already had the cauliflower-and-broccoli cheese bake on her plate. Our two families had spent most of July in a five-star hotel near my aunt's small apartment in Vouliagmeni, courtesy of Solomon Daisy and Mannasoft Games. Crina's sun-lightened hair was almost blonde. She had kept it short and bought a new pair of glasses with gold rims that matched her Greek suntan.

She also had a new pin on the lapel of her blazer: a tiny white enamel butterfly. I had bought it for her on the last day of our hols.

'What's going on there?' I tipped my head towards the mass of admirers.

Crina rolled her eyes. 'Britney's older brother was on *Love Island*. And now everyone wants to know more about him and the girl he hooked up with. I'm afraid you and Dinu are old news.'

I got into the queue for food behind Dinu and said, 'Looks like our fifteen minutes of fame are over, dude.'

'Thank God.'

Once the dinner ladies had given me and Dinu beef lasagne and garlic bread, we took our trays and looked for somewhere to sit.

The Mean Girls' table was full and they were too busy discussing Britney's brother to notice us. I saw my former girlfriend Kiana sitting next to a Polish boy named Filip, star of the school's top football team. Their heads were close together and she didn't even see me go past.

I felt a small pang, but consoled myself with the thought that we didn't really have that much in common.

Also, she'd only liked me because I was 'popular'.

Relieved to no longer be the object of everyone's attention, Dinu and I headed for the back of the cafeteria, looking for a free table.

We chose one by a window.

'So are you and your gran going to use your millions to get a new flat?' Dinu put down his tray and pulled out a chair.

'Probably not.' I sat across from him. 'We donated half of it to a charity and Gran put the rest in a trust fund that can only be accessed when I go to university. She won't even give me an allowance. She says I need to get an after-school job.'

A girl sat down beside me. It was Crina.

'What's this?' I raised an eyebrow in mock surprise. 'A Year Eight girl sitting with Year Nine geeks?'

'Why not? We don't care what people think, do we?' She reached across me for the shaker of Parmesan cheese. 'So did Dinu tell you what he did with his millions?'

'No!' I looked at my best friend.

Dinu had changed since we got back from Greece. He was starting to get spots and also some fuzz on his upper lip, so he wasn't quite as pretty as he had been half a year ago.

But there was something else different about him.

Although he didn't joke as much as he used to, he seemed happier somehow.

He now had a kind of Zen calm.

You might even call it *eudaimonia*.

'So, Mr Moneybags,' I asked him, 'what did you do with your fortune? Give it away to charity?'

Dinu gave a half-smile. 'I bought a workshop for my father.'

'You bought a workshop? What kind of workshop?'

'Carpentry. When we lived in Romania, he used to make furniture as a hobby. But he never had much time for it. Last week we found a good workshop across the river in Chelsea. Our offer was accepted yesterday.'

'Papa is a brilliant carpenter.' Crina was tapping the bottom of the Parmesan, trying to get the cheese to loosen up. 'He's going to make bespoke furniture and our mother will do cushions and things. They'll sell their stuff online, or people can come into the workshop. It's really nice and bright with a big skylight.'

'Did the workshop cost the whole ten mil?' I asked Dinu.

'Course not. We're using the rest to buy a nice flat by the river.'

Suddenly I wasn't hungry any more.

## 57
# Socrates Club

Were my best friends about to move away, thanks to their newfound wealth?

I put down my fork. 'Where?' I said, my appetite gone. 'Where are you moving to?'

'Probably right here in Wandsworth,' said Crina, still tapping the Parmesan shaker. 'We like this area.'

'There's a new riverside development not far from you,' said Dinu. 'It's called Smuggler's Wharf. It's really nice.'

I knew Smuggler's Wharf. It was only a five-minute walk from our flat. My appetite revived and I tucked into my lasagne. 'That sounds like a good use of Daisy's millions.'

'It is,' said Dinu. 'It means my father will be around all the time. Oh, and I bought four season tickets to Fulham.'

'Fulham? That's my team!' I narrowed my eyes at him. 'I thought you and your dad supported Liverpool. Nobody changes allegiance. Ever.'

'We still support Liverpool. But it's too far to go often, and that doesn't mean we can't attend local matches too. Do you want to go with us next Saturday?'

'*Day-lon hotee*,' I replied with a grin. Of course.

I tipped my head towards Crina and raised my eyebrows at Dinu.

'Oh, I already asked her. She doesn't want to come.'

Crina had finally got the Parmesan dispenser to work and was shaking it over her cheese bake. 'No football for me,' she said briskly. 'I have a protest march on Saturday.' She changed the subject. 'Did Dinu tell you that he's also quite good at carpentry?'

'Really?' I raised my eyebrows.

'Yeah,' said Dinu, holding out his hand for the cheese. 'I'm going to help in the workshop when I have time. I've already got a design for a chair.'

'An ideal chair, I hope.' Crina gave me a playful nudge with her elbow.

I grinned. 'I think Kid Plato was the one who came up with the concept of the Forms. When he was Old Plato,' I added.

'We could discuss the ideal chair at the new club.' Crina handed Dinu the Parmesan.

'Club? What club?' Dinu shook cheese onto his pasta.

'Our new Socrates club.'

I turned to look at her. 'But I thought you were going to join our Latin club?'

'I am. Latin club on Tuesdays and Socrates club on Thursdays. Dr Stewart says we can use his classroom if we get at least six kids to sign up. And he can even get funding for textbooks if we do a little ancient Greek.'

'It sounds cool,' I said. 'I'm in. You up for that, Dinu?'

Dinu chewed thoughtfully. Then his eyes widened as a Year Eight girl named Hope sat down beside him.

Hope is in Crina's class. Her mum is Japanese and her dad is from Portugal. She has silky black hair and intense dark eyes, and Crina says she's bright as well as beautiful.

'Are you coming to our Socrates club, Dinu?' she asked him.

Dinu nearly choked on his lasagne. 'You're joining the Socrates club?'

'Yes!' said Hope brightly. 'Crina told me about it. It sounds really interesting. Plus it will look good on my list of extra-curricular activities.'

'Hope wants to be a doctor,' Crina explained. 'She's got it all planned out.'

Before Dinu could answer, a Year Ten boy from Latin club put down his tray. Some kids call him Sam Solo because he loves *Star Wars* and usually sits on his own.

'I hear you're starting a philosophy club,' he said, straightening his knife and fork. 'May I join?'

'Sure!' said Crina. 'Only we're calling it the Socrates club.'

'Good,' said Sam. 'I like Socrates. Also Plato. But Aristotle is my favourite.'

'Great!' said Crina. 'My idea is that we'll discuss topics using the Socratic method. We can ask each other questions instead of just stating what we believe. Sometimes we might not actually find an answer. But it's the discussion that would be important. Hearing each other's points of view. Being willing to admit we don't always have the answers. What do you think?'

'*Love Island!*' said a familiar voice. It was Chastity, the prettiest Mean Girl of them all. She was standing behind me and Crina with a fruit-cup dessert. Her fair hair was no longer blue-tipped but I could still see the butterfly tattoo on her neck.

'Wrong table,' Crina said.

I added, 'We're talking about a Socrates club.'

'I know,' she said brightly, and pulled up a chair. 'We could use the Socratic method to discuss the ethical implications of glorifying fake tans and plastic bodies. It would tie in with Plato's concepts of the Beautiful, don't you think?'

We stared at her, open-mouthed.

All except for Sam, who said, 'But we'd have to define what is beautiful first.'

'Naturally.' Chastity gave him a dazzling smile. 'Socrates wouldn't have it any other way.'

I looked at Dinu. 'So are you in?' I asked. 'We only need one more.'

He grinned and shrugged. 'I'm not clever like the rest of you,' he said, 'but why not? I have the perfect qualification.'

'What's that?' we all asked.

'*Oo-den oy-dah.*' I know nothing.

*The end*

# AUTHOR'S NOTE

L ike Alex and Dinu's previous adventure, this story is completely made up. Lots of it is based on literary sources, especially Plato's dialogues, which are famous accounts of Socrates and his philosophy. However, until someone invents a time machine for real, we will never know how accurate Plato's accounts really were.

What we do know about the bug-eyed, bearded, snub-nosed, wide-mouthed philosopher named Socrates is that he changed the world forever, especially the way we think. Philosophers before him are called 'Pre-Socratics' and philosophers after him always kept him in mind.

Two thousand years ago, the Roman philosopher and statesman Cicero wrote, 'All philosophers think of themselves, and want others to think of them, as followers of Socrates.'

More recently a modern philosopher named Scott Samuelson wrote, 'I put myself in that long line of philosophers who believe Socrates the wisest, most happy, most just man who ever lived. What Mozart is to music, Socrates is to being human.'

The Socrates in Plato's dialogues is Plato's version. The Socrates in Xenophon's histories is Xenophon's version. The same with Aristophanes, Diogenes Laertius and many other authors who have written about him.

What I did to create my version of Socrates was to read lots of books about him but especially the primary sources – that is, books written in ancient times by people who actually knew him. I even read some of those primary sources in ancient Greek (which nearly did my head in!).

Then I took all those facts and bits of information and used my imagination to create my own Socrates.

If time travel existed, I would love to go back 2,435 years or so to ancient Athens and follow Socrates to see how he interacted with people. But time travel will probably never happen, so in the meantime our imaginations are the best portals we have to the past.

And stories are the best way I know of telling people what's important.

# Caroline Lawrence

Caroline Lawrence's Roman Mysteries books were first published in 2001 and have since sold over a million copies in the UK alone, and been translated into fourteen languages. The series was televised by the BBC in 2007 and 2008 with ten half-hour episodes per season. Filmed in Tunisia, Bulgaria and Malta, it was the most expensive BBC children's TV series to date.

Caroline says: 'I want to know everything about the past, especially the exciting things. Also the sounds, smells, sights and tastes. I write historical novels because nobody has invented a Time Machine. And I write for kids because eleven is my inner age.'

Visit Caroline's website: www.carolinelawrence.com

Look out for

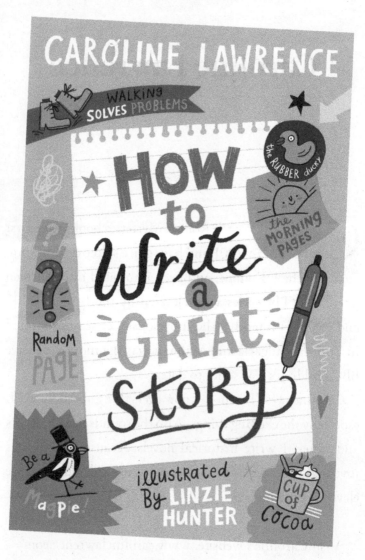

Piccadilly
PRESS